CAMP TROUBLE

CAMP TROUBLE

BEVERLY KELLER

AN
APPLE
PAPERBACK

SCHOLASTIC INC.
New York Toronto London Auckland Sydney

ISBN 0-590-43728-3

12 11 10 9 8 7 6 5 4   0/0

Printed in the U.S.A.   40
First Scholastic printing, May 1993

To Grace Schultz

CAMP TROUBLE

1

The minute she sat down to dinner, Phoebe Townsend-Fanchon saw that something was wrong. Her carrots were large and limp and whole. Her green beans still had a few stray pod strings on them. *Someone had gone to the trouble of cooking fresh vegetables!*

For one of Phoebe's parents to serve anything that did not come from a carton, or a can, or a take-out place was almost unheard of. "Would you please pass the — are those *real* mashed potatoes, not the kind from a box?" she asked her father cautiously.

Iris Townsend, Phoebe's mother, began turning her wedding ring around on her finger, the way she always did when she was uncomfortable.

Iris Townsend did not look like a person who became uncomfortable easily. She was a tall woman with a long face and big dark eyes. When she was playing in a concert, she wore long, flowing dresses, with her black hair coiled at the nape of her neck. When she was not in a concert, she wore clothes that looked like something a woman explorer would have worn on a jungle expedition in 1910.

Phoebe knew that her parents were not like other parents. They spent their working hours in a converted warehouse near the waterfront, Iris practicing the piano, Brian the violin. In one section of the warehouse, a sculptor had his studio, where he made metal statues with a blowtorch. In another section was a painter who used only natural materials, like tar and berry juices. Phoebe had seen the sculptor and the painter the few times her parents brought her to the warehouse, but she wasn't allowed to speak to them.

"They can't stand children," her mother had explained.

Sometimes, Phoebe could not help wondering what it might be like to have parents who watched football games and drove a station wagon.

Mainly, Phoebe imagined having parents who cooked regularly. When they were playing a lot of concert dates, the Townsend-Fanchons had a housekeeper. When the housekeeper moved on, or the Townsend-Fanchons ran out of money, meals got weird around the apartment.

Even at ten, Phoebe knew that other parents do not open a can of smoked mushrooms, a box of Table Water Crackers, and a couple of bottles of Perrier water and call it lunch. Nor do they shake out a few soy protein tablets and call them dessert.

"Phoebe," Brian Fanchon began now, "your mother and I have been talking."

That was another thing, Phoebe thought. Neither of her parents had ever been married before, and she was their only child. But Iris Townsend kept her unmarried name. Phoebe could not help thinking it would be rather cozy to have parents who shared a last name.

"We decided you might like to go to summer camp," her father continued.

Phoebe set down the basket of ten-grain rolls, stunned. The worst she had expected was to be left with a hired sitter while her parents were on tour. But to be shipped off to the *wilderness* was something so unthinkable it hadn't even occurred to her.

Every July, Heather Bowen and Tiffany Reilly, who lived across the street, went to Camp Big Tree. Every August they came home with poison oak and sunburn. Every August they came home even more obnoxious than before.

"I talked to Heather's and Tiffany's mothers," Iris Townsend said. "We thought it would be great fun for you three girls to all go together."

"Fun? *Fun?*" Phoebe was stunned. "The best weeks of my *life* are in July, when they're both at that Big Tree. Mother, they are *twelve*. They never let me forget I'm only ten. They never let me forget we rent an apartment and their parents *own* their houses. They make horrible jokes about my name."

Her mother leaned toward her, looking concerned. "Phoebe is a beautiful name."

"Mother, how would you like being called Feeble?"

"Dear," Iris Townsend said gently, "you must learn not to be so sensitive."

Phoebe realized she was letting her parents dodge the main issue. "I wouldn't be any trouble on the road. I could read in the hotel rooms. I could improve my mind."

"Phoebe," her father said reasonably, "we went over this months ago. A concert tour is an ordeal even for the artists. To bring a child along would be impossible. It would be *cruel*."

Phoebe let the tears roll down her face. Why worry about making parents feel guilty when they double-cross you like this? "And not even my own *grandmother* wants me!"

Iris Townsend leaned over to dab Phoebe's tears with a table napkin. "Sweetheart, your grandmother has kept you every year when we toured. This year she is taking a cruise. She may even have a gentleman friend."

"Mother, don't be gross!" Phoebe was shocked. Her grandmother was at least sixty.

Iris Townsend and Brian Fanchon did not seem nearly as upset as parents who are destroying

4

their child's whole life should be.

Phoebe let her voice go low and pitiful. "Nobody wants me around because I'm pale and skinny and wear stupid glasses."

"Phoebe! Phoebe! Phoebe!" Her father came around the table, knocking over the carafe of Evian spring water. "You are just a little overly *slender*. Your face is *interesting*. When you're old enough, we'll buy you contact lenses."

Iris Townsend stroked Phoebe's hand. "Besides, looks don't matter."

Phoebe gazed bleakly at her mother and father.

If they refused to accept any responsibility for producing such a medium-looking kid, she thought, how could you expect them to feel any qualms about dumping her at some camp? Instead of her mother's dark hair and eyes and impressive carriage, Phoebe had got her father's build and coloring and unaggressive air. She was just a little under average height. Her eyes were the same light hazel as her father's, her hair the same straight medium brown. Once in a while she wondered if it would start going thin around the temples like his, when she was in her thirties.

Her parents would go on this tour, she knew. That was how they made a living.

If they were rock stars instead of classical musicians, she thought, at least they would be famous, and everybody would want to know me.

Nobody would make fun of my name, or put me down for being ten and living in a rented apartment.

"Sweetheart," her mother said, "it's only two weeks at camp. And you will learn to love it."

"Did you?"

"Oh, I . . . I've never been to one." Iris blotted the Evian water with Brian's napkin. "Whenever school was out, I practiced the piano five hours a day. That's what you must do if you're going to be a pianist."

Phoebe looked at her father.

"I missed a lot, never going to camp," he said. "But my parents were nervous about my hurting my fingers. If you're going to play the violin seriously — "

"You get out of dumb things like summer camp," Phoebe finished.

"Sweetheart," Iris said firmly, "the last time we left you with a sitter from the agency, we came home to find a week's dishes in the sink alive with fuzzy gray mold. We found hideous mummified slices of abandoned pizza between the sofa cushions. She bleached her hair with something that ate the enamel off the bathroom basin. We are sending you to Big Blossom because we love you."

"Big Tree," Phoebe muttered. "And I . . ."

Iris kissed Phoebe's forehead. "You're signed up for the next session. It starts in a week. We've ordered you lovely camping clothes and rushed all

6

the arrangements for the tour just so we can devote all the next days to you."

"A week!" Phoebe cried. "You had the whole thing all set up!"

"No, dear," her mother said. "We had it *arranged*."

If they paid for the two weeks in advance, Phoebe thought hopelessly, there may be no way out of this.

"Okay." If she was doomed, she might as well try to salvage what she could. "How about a deal? Suppose I go peacefully? Suppose I suffer through this? And you let me change my name."

"My lamb." Iris Townsend stroked Phoebe's hair. "We've been over and over this. If you change your name, and then somebody tacky or peculiar comes up with the same name, you'll want to change yours again. You could end up with an identity problem."

Brian Fanchon kissed Phoebe's cheek. "You wouldn't want parents you could blackmail like that. You wouldn't respect us."

2

In the morning, Iris Townsend found the camp's brochure, which she had misplaced under the overdue bills, on her desk.

She curled up on the window seat beside Phoebe, who was staring out at the soft San Francisco summer fog.

"Here we are." Being nearsighted, Iris held the pamphlet too close to Phoebe's face. BIG TREE was printed in red block letters on its front, under a picture of a log cabin with a few scrubby stunted pines behind it.

Gazing at the photo, Phoebe could imagine the people who started the camp having a meeting to decide what to call it. "Whole lot of dirt?" somebody probably suggested. "No," everybody said. "Bunch of dead weeds?" "Nah." "Wait . . . how about . . . how about Big Tree? In fifty or sixty years the name might fit."

Phoebe's mother unfolded the pamphlet. Inside was a snapshot of a skimpy, murky lake.

"It looks like the kind of lake where teenagers go camping, and a maniac murders them one by one," Phoebe muttered.

Iris Townsend's lips tightened, but she unfolded the pamphlet again. "Look at all the activities. Archery . . ."

"It's probably full of pond sharks, anyway."

"*Pond sharks?*"

"There are sand sharks, aren't there? If you can get sharks in sand, you can sure get them in a pond that big. I've heard of them."

Iris Townsend closed her eyes for a moment. But she kept her voice calm. "And here. *Riding.*" She showed Phoebe a snapshot of a grim-looking girl sitting on a swaybacked downcast horse.

Phoebe shook her head. "Imagine making a horse in *that* condition spend his life hauling people around on his back."

Iris Townsend refolded the camp brochure all wrong, slapped it into Phoebe's hand, and stood up. "You can be as negative as you like, Phoebe Townsend-Fanchon, but you are still going to this camp!"

The day before Phoebe was to leave for Big Tree, she and her mother picked up the clothes and the name tags Iris had ordered. Then they bought Phoebe a pair of tall, round-toed, low-heeled English riding boots.

She can't have any notions about my riding horses, Phoebe reassured herself. She must just want me to have boots so I can sit around the bonfires looking like the other campers.

That evening, Iris Townsend laid out the clothes on her bed.

They must have gotten a bank loan, or an advance payment for the tour, Phoebe mused. Now they've blown it all on the camp and these clothes, so we'll be back to living off whatever food they can buy on credit cards at Cost Plus or Long's Drugs.

She picked up a pair of heavy pants. "These pooch way out at the sides."

"That's how jodhpurs are *made*." Iris held a checked wool jacket up to Phoebe's chest. "Won't this be smashing with them? You're going to look just like the riders in all the horse shows."

"Mama, I don't even want to get *close* to a horse! They snort! They roll their eyes! They have teeth the size of piano keys!"

"Sweetheart, every girl should learn to ride. I want you to have the advantages I missed."

"*Ride? Ride?* Mama, *why*? When have you ever seen anybody but a police officer ride a horse in San Francisco?"

"Ah, here's your father."

Brian Fanchon had brought home half a dozen cartons of Japanese take-out food.

If they ever cut off our credit cards, Phoebe thought, we'll starve.

After dinner, Brian began ironing name tags on Phoebe's shirts and socks, and even the towels she was going to take.

Iris Townsend packed the tagged items in her old Gucci suitcases. "I am sure one does not take new luggage to camp," she announced. "It would look so gauche. Besides, well-aged Guccis can go anywhere."

"Goesh?" Phoebe had no idea what the word meant, but she had an idea she didn't want to look whatever it was.

"Gauche. Tacky," Iris explained. "As if you've never been to camp before."

"Mother, I *haven't* ever been to camp before."

"But there's no point announcing it," her mother said.

Phoebe watched her father press her clothes. "It's a lot of work just to ship your kid off to suffer for two weeks."

Her mother did not look up from packing. "Campers have to have their tags on everything they bring. If we didn't put your name on your belongings, how would you tell them from all the others?"

"Mine would be the ones without tags."

Her mother looked up, then. "Why don't you get ready for bed?"

Her parents were still ironing and packing when Phoebe kissed them good night.

In the morning, a San Francisco summer mist hid all the houses across the street, the tall lavender and blue Victorian that Heather's family lived in — and owned — and the gray and white Victorian that Tiffany's family lived in — and owned.

Phoebe put on the new khaki slacks with pockets over the knees and the African camp shirt and saddle shoes set out for her. She was too depressed to object when Iris made her take *The Family Medical Guide* out of her suitcase.

At breakfast, Phoebe ignored the vitamin tablet by her plate. "*The Family Medical Guide* says that bare dirt, like you'd find around a horse barn, is full of tetanus viruses."

"Tetanus is a bacteria, not a virus." Her father poured himself a glass of mango juice.

"A person could step on a horseshoe nail and be gone like *that*."

"You've had all your tetanus boosters," Iris assured her.

"Have I ever had a dangerous reaction to any bites?" Phoebe asked. "*The Family Medical Guide* says to watch out for that."

Her mother stirred a spoonful of honey into a cup of Celestial Seasonings Red Zinger tea. "Bites?"

"You know — bees, wasps, rattlesnakes . . ."

Brian Fanchon set down his glasses. "Phoebe, there will not be rattlesnakes at camp. Rattlesnakes *avoid* people."

Phoebe spread almond butter on her amaranth toast. "You can't trust an animal with rabies to avoid people."

"Snakes do not get rabies," her father said firmly. "Only warm-blooded animals get rabies, and I don't think we need to discuss fatal illnesses at breakfast."

There was no way out, now. Phoebe knew that if she cried, they would comfort her, but still send her to camp.

"Okay. I know you're going to make me go. I know that. Just don't make me ride a horse."

Her father blotted tea off his moustache. "Muffin, nobody's going to force you to ride anything."

"So you can just return the horse show clothes you bought me."

"Of course we can't," her mother said. "How would it look if we sent you to camp with no riding gear? You would look deprived."

Brian Fanchon smiled. "Besides, once you get there you'll want to do what all the other girls do."

The fog was blowing away when Phoebe saw

from her window the Bowen's blue sedan pulling into her driveway.

She stood still while her father kissed her. Then she picked up the smaller Gucci case and followed her mother out to the car.

Heather and Tiffany huddled on the back seat wearing jeans and sneakers and plaid shirts, whispering together and giggling.

"All ready?" Mrs. Bowen got out of the car and walked around to unlock the trunk. Even living in San Francisco, she kept a tan all year. This morning she wore a green shirt, flared beige skirt, and low-heeled beige pumps.

Phoebe's mother, still in her old Cost Plus caftan, hoisted the big Gucci bag into the trunk.

"Suitcases!" Tiffany squealed and covered her mouth.

Phoebe put the smaller Gucci bag into the trunk next to two nylon backpacks, two full duffel bags, and two rolled sleeping bags. On top of the sleeping bags were two pairs of cowboy boots with tall heels and pointed toes.

I could say I am carsick, Phoebe thought, but I haven't even gotten into the car. I could say I am coming down with something. Then my mother or father would stay home from the tour, waiting for me to get sick with what I was coming down with. They would never forgive me when I didn't. If only one of them couldn't go, they'd still have to cancel the tour. Then we'd have no way to pay any of our bills. They'd probably not even *listen* next time I asked to change my name.

Iris Townsend enveloped Phoebe in a hug. "You'll have a wonderful time, sweetheart."

As soon as she could get free without hurting her mother's feelings, Phoebe hurried to the back door of the sedan.

Heather and Tiffany spread out their arms and legs so that there was no room.

Mrs. Bowen opened the front door on the passenger side, and Phoebe climbed into the front seat.

As they pulled away, Phoebe leaned her head back, hoping her tears would drain back into her tear ducts at the corners of her eyes and everyone would think she was just resting her skull.

"Don't you hate it the way little kids get all snuffly and sniffly and weepy when they go away from home?" Tiffany muttered.

Mrs. Bowen ignored her. "You'll like Camp Big Tree," she assured Phoebe. "The Perrys have done wonders with it. Do you remember them?"

"Her?" Heather sniffed, "She's only *ten*."

Mrs. Bowen went on talking to Phoebe. "When I was a little girl, they made dozens of movies. Then, five or six years ago they had that local television show. It was mostly their movies chopped up into serial episodes, but sometimes

Cowboy Hank Perry would sing and play the guitar. And Lady Lou Perry did the commercials for some dreadful milk flavoring."

"Yummoo," Heather put in.

"Yummoo," Mrs. Bowen said, as if her daughter hadn't spoken. "I bought it once. It settled at the bottom of the glass in great disgusting globs."

"I just hope the Perrys don't see us drive up with old Feeble," Heather told Tiffany. "I mean, they send us a *Christmas* card every year."

"They send *everybody* Christmas cards," Tiffany told her coldly.

3

How *ow can it be a whole different climate when*
we're only an hour from San Francisco?
Itchy from the heat, dizzy from the sun, Phoebe
stood in front of a long log cabin that had a wooden
sign over the door reading TOWN HALL. On the
porch was a redwood picnic table, and before it a
line of girls straggled all the way down the stairs
and onto the dusty parking lot.

The heat was not the worst of it. At the edge
of the lot, about fifty yards to the left of the cabin
stood four enormous wooden wagons. Hitched to
each was a huge, heavy-boned horse.

Sure, they look bored, Phoebe thought. Sure,
they show no signs of life. But everybody knows
animals sense how a person feels. Let some kid
like me get too close and they'll rear right up at
her.

Girls in blue jeans and sneakers and T-shirts
were tossing sleeping bags and duffel bags and
high-heeled, pointy-toed boots into the wagons.

17

Some were even petting the horses. It only reinforced Phoebe's suspicion that people who went to camp were a wild and reckless lot, and that horses sensed how people felt. Any kid who would walk right up and touch a horse plainly had no fear. Or no sense.

The campers seemed to range in age from six or seven to over twelve, but there was not a suitcase in sight, not a pair of khaki slacks or saddle shoes.

Mrs. Bowen beside her, Heather and Tiffany behind her, Phoebe moved forward in line, scooting the bags along with her feet, then lifting them step to step. Just because I'm moving them doesn't necessarily mean people will think they're mine, she told herself. I could be just keeping an eye on them as a favor for some poor dumb kid whose parents didn't know you take duffel bags and backpacks to camp.

A square-faced woman with frizzy blonde hair sat on the bench behind the table. Below the pocket of her plaid shirt was a stick-on badge that had CYPRESS printed on it.

Sitting on either side of her were two girls who looked to be about sixteen. One wore a badge that read SUMAC, and the other wore one that read LAUREL. Laurel was tall and wiry, with short curly brown hair and a faint moustache over her upper lip. Sumac was short and chunky, so blonde her hair and her eyelashes were almost white.

Reaching the head of the line, Mrs. Bowen announced, "Phoebe Townsend-Fanchon, and Tiffany Reilly, and of course you know my Heather."

It's not too late. I could say, "I'm sorry. This has all been a terrible mistake. I have this pain building up right here under my navel, which, according to The Family Medical Guide, *is one of the first warning signs of appendicitis."*

Without looking up, Cypress flipped through the papers on the clipboard. "Townsend, Fanchon, Reilly, Bowen."

Laurel pawed through a plastic tray full of stick-on badges and drew out three. "We've got Townsend and Fanchon on one badge."

"It's one person." Mrs. Bowen handed Heather and Tiffany their badges, then peeled the back off the third, and stuck it on Phoebe's shirt.

"One Feeble person." As her mother glared at her, Heather picked up her gear and strolled toward the wagons, Tiffany following.

"You go along while I talk to the counselors," Mrs. Bowen told Phoebe. "I'll bring your big bag."

What do you say to the mother of a kid who torments you? No? "I would rather throw up, right here, in my own shoes than walk over to those wagons alone in front of everybody, carrying a suitcase and wearing saddle shoes and khaki slacks with knee pockets?"

You don't say anything. You walk as fast as you can without attracting attention. You keep your

19

eyes on the ground, remembering that when you were very little you could almost convince yourself that if you didn't look at people they couldn't see you.

Phoebe got to the closest wagon just as Heather and Tiffany were heaving their belongings into it.

"Not *this* wagon, Feeble," Tiffany told her. "Find your own!"

"Here." Coming up behind Phoebe, Heather's mother hoisted the big bag into the wagon. Then she took the smaller one from Phoebe and tossed it in.

"You two," she told Heather and Tiffany sternly. "There will be no more of this Feeble business, and no teasing, you understand? I asked the counselors to put you three girls in the same tent, so you can look after Phoebe."

"*Mother!*" Heather wailed.

"*Guy!*" Tiffany set her teeth and rolled her eyes skyward.

"You will be nice to her. That's an order." Mrs. Bowen hugged Phoebe, then Heather and Tiffany, and walked away, the dust swirling around her legs.

I could run after her, Phoebe thought. I could say I forgot to send my grandmother a birthday present.

My grandmother's birthday is in January.

I could say I am on lifesaving medication, which I forgot to bring with me.

She's getting into her car!

I could run after her and yell that I cannot be left here. If I fell down in the dust and poured dirt over my hair, she would see that I sincerely meant it.

And it would give Heather and Tiffany something to torture me about for years.

Phoebe watched Mrs. Bowen pull away.

"This is the pits, isn't it?"

Phoebe turned.

"I'm Amy." The girl who had spoken was about Phoebe's age, a couple of inches shorter and at least twenty pounds heavier. Her face was round, her eyes were pale blue and she already wore braces on her teeth. Her hair was tan, short and limp. But even this kid wore jeans, and a T-shirt, and sneakers.

She stood beside Phoebe looking up at her like a stray dog that would follow anybody, friendly, hopeful, and a little bit anxious. I know what will happen, Phoebe thought. This kid is going to attach herself to me. This Amy has sized me up as another loser.

The girl went on talking, as if afraid Phoebe might forget she was there. "What's your name?"

"Phoebe."

"This is my third year," Amy said. "My parents

say the exercise burns weight off me. I do come home thinner, but it's the food, not the exercise. Parents never listen when you tell them what they don't want to hear, though."

Phoebe was careful not to seem interested. If I give her any encouragement, she thought, I will never get rid of her.

"So how long are you here for?" Amy seemed afraid that if she let the conversation die, Phoebe would walk away.

Even if I don't encourage her, Phoebe realized, I may have trouble getting rid of her. "Two weeks."

"Me, too. Last summer it was for four, but they hiked the prices this year."

By now, all the other girls had climbed into the wagons.

"Everybody in!" Laurel, in the closest wagon, commanded.

Heather and Tiffany gazed down at Phoebe like cats waiting for a mouse to join them.

"Listen, hang on. I'll be right back!" To Phoebe's relief, Amy turned and trotted back toward Town Hall.

The horse is at the other end of the wagon, Phoebe told herself. The horse has no personal interest at all in who gets in. She put her foot on the wheel nearest her, but the soles of her new shoes were still slippery. She hung on to the wagon side, even though her palms were wet. If the horse starts running, and I'm flung off, I might get hurt bad enough to be sent home, she thought, even as she struggled for a foothold. Nothing bad like a fracture. Maybe just a slight concussion. But the way things are going, I'd be more likely just to get dumped in the dust in my slacks and saddle shoes in front of everybody.

She clambered into the wagon.

"Who's the kid in the safari outfit?" she heard a camper ask.

A minute later, the three horses on the right began plodding forward.

"Wait up! Hold on!" Amy came running from the Town Hall.

"Oh, for Pete's sake!" Laurel jumped down, came around behind her, and gave her a great shove.

Amy landed in the cart on both elbows.

Heather and Tiffany and the other girls in the wagon greeted her.

"*Watch it!*"

"*Look out!*"

"*Klutz!*"

Laurel took her seat, and the wagon started with a lurch.

The other girls in the wagon ignored Amy and Phoebe.

At least these campers have a short attention span, Phoebe consoled herself. If I don't do anything to attract their attention, they may just overlook me for the next two weeks.

Two weeks. Something has to happen to get me out of here. There is no way I can survive two weeks in this place.

Amy got her breath back. "Well, I fixed it. I got them to put us in the same tent."

I knew it, Phoebe thought in despair. I knew it! She's going to stick like bubble gum in hair.

But as the horses ambled along a dirt path, and Amy kept talking at her, Phoebe had time to consider things. Having this kid in the tent means one less friend of Heather and Tiffany's. And this Amy is plainly a person who attracts teasing, so at least I won't get it all.

Phoebe gazed through the dust at the tan stubble on the land. They definitely should have named it Bunch of Dead Weeds, she mused.

She rode on, trying to imagine things that might deliver her from this place, things nobody could suspect her of doing. A plague of sinister spider bites that would cause the camp to be closed. An earthquake, just enough to have Big Tree evacuated, without actually hurting anything. An order from the state that because of drought, the camp would have to conserve water by sending everybody home.

Then she saw that the drought was not a possibility.

Ahead and to her right was a wide, deep green

lawn glittering with the water from half a dozen sprinklers. Set well back from the road was a long, low, white-painted house with a veranda running all along the front of it.

"That's where the Perrys live," Amy told her.

A small woman in a white embroidered shirt, divided skirt, and white cowboy boots stood on the veranda. Her hair was an astonishing bright yellow, and her vest so covered with beads and fringe that she looked as if she were encrusted with barnacles. A short, stocky man stood beside her, his hair as black as if it had been painted on, and his vest even more fringed and beaded than hers.

From all the wagons came squeals and shrieks.

"It's Lady Lou and Cowboy Hank!"

"They looked at me!"

"They're waving!"

Cowboy Hank and Lady Lou were, indeed, waving. Their right arms were bent and raised at the elbow, and their right hands moved side to side like metronomes.

"You know what they remind me of?" Amy whispered. "Those robots at Disneyland. And this is about as close as they get to any kids."

Phoebe had never visited Disneyland. She had been to the Ashland Shakespeare Festival and the Opera on the Green, she had been to so many Christmas performances of *The Nutcracker* that the mere thought of Sugar Plum Fairies turned her stomach, but she had never been to Disneyland.

Nevertheless, watching the Perrys, she could see that they did, indeed, have a spooky resemblance to robots.

As the wagons jounced on, the green lawn gave way to more tan dirt and weeds.

Then, to the left, Phoebe saw a corral the size of a city block, with over a dozen horses standing around, looking casual, like a wolf pack waiting for a moose to blunder by.

"Oh, boy."

Amy looked at her. "What?"

"The horses. They're . . . large." This was no time to be worried about seeming too friendly — not when you're the only kid wearing a safari outfit. With everybody else in the wagon chattering on about the Perrys, there was no need to worry about being overheard, either. "Listen, I've got this grandmother on a cruise ship. Say a person was really desperate. Do you suppose they could send a helicopter out from the ship to pick her up?"

Amy looked solemn. "Do you know what that would *cost*?"

"A lot?"

"A *fortune*," Amy said firmly. "And what about hurricanes?"

"Hurricanes?"

"A 'copter would drop like a stone in a hurricane."

Though she was shaken, Phoebe was not ready to give up. "What makes you think they're having a hurricane where my grandmother's ship is?"

"Summer is when hurricanes happen. And they move, you know."

She may be a loser, Phoebe thought, but she knows things. Even this kid could be better than not having a single friend in the place.

"So you live with your grandmother, or what?" Amy asked.

"No. But with her on a cruise, my folks didn't have anyplace else to send me. They're going on tour."

A couple of girls turned, suddenly interested and respectful.

Amy looked impressed. "Tour? What group are they in?"

For a second, Phoebe was tempted. But then she realized that the stress of carrying on a pretense was more than she could handle for a day, let alone two weeks. "Not rock, classical. My father's a violinist and my mother's a pianist."

The older girls went on talking to each other, each claiming her parents were close personal friends of the Perrys.

"Oh." Amy looked disappointed, but only for a

second. "I thought they might be somebody famous. But, listen, that's okay. I bet they're very good."

"You live with your parents?" Phoebe asked.

Amy nodded. "And my big brother. He's in high school, but he's not too bad. We live down the peninsula, in Belmont."

"So do both your parents have the same last name?"

Amy looked only faintly surprised. "Sure. Neither of them has been married before."

Phoebe nodded. "Do they both work?"

"They have a carpet store."

"But they don't have to go away on business a lot."

"Never," Amy said.

"They drive a station wagon, or what?"

"They have a sedan, and a van for the business." Amy looked at Phoebe closely. "I never knew a kid who was so interested in *parents* before."

"They just seemed to me like people who'd have a station wagon," Phoebe said.

The horses stopped in front of a long, unpainted building with a corrugated tin roof.

"The mess hall," Amy said. "You can see why the brochures never show a picture of it. The only stuff that looks authentic is the stuff parents see when they drive up."

Between the wagons and the mess hall was a

large, shallow pit half full of ashes and charred logs.

"What's *that*?" Even though she knew better, Phoebe couldn't help thinking of burnings at the stake.

"The firepit." Amy climbed out of the wagon. "Haven't you ever been to a cookout?"

Phoebe looked at the debris in the pit and the dust around it. "We generally like to eat where it's clean."

As the last people piled out of the wagon, Phoebe hesitated. If I could be absolutely sure no hurricanes were coming up, she thought, I could say I have to run back to the mess hall and make an emergency call. But how do you phone a ship at sea, collect?

Laurel marched to the front of the mess hall, where six other teenage girls stood looking as warm and full of fun as suspects in a police lineup.

Phoebe stayed with Amy at the back of the crowd of campers, as far from Heather and Tiffany as she could get.

"Listen up, guys!" Laurel's voice was hearty. "These are your counselors. You met Cypress when you signed in. Next to me are Sumac, Pine, and Birch. On my other side are Alder, Oak, and Juniper."

They may not look friendly, Phoebe mused, but they don't look actively *hostile*, either. They're probably feeling a lot of responsibility. Counselors are people who advise you, people you can talk to. Maybe they'll give me one who'll turn out to be like a friend.

"You notice they're all named for trees or bushes?" she whispered. "They must be related. Or else it's really a weird coincidence."

Two girls in front of her turned around and snickered.

"Those aren't their real names," Amy murmured. "Those are their *camp* names."

Phoebe could feel her face go hot from embarrassment. At least Amy didn't laugh at me, she thought. But I'd better keep my mouth shut until I learn my way around here.

"Rules!" Laurel announced. "Breakfast is at seven, mail call at eleven, lunch at eleven forty-five, dinner at five, lights out at nine. And wherever you are, never wander off into the brush. We keep the paths and the areas where you belong clear of poison oak, but there's no way we can kill it off in the whole camp."

It would be a lot nicer if they started out with "Welcome," Phoebe mused, and then something like, "If you have any problems, your counselor is here to help you."

"There'll be six campers and one counselor to a tent. After you stow your belongings, I want you back here." As Laurel began reading off names from the list on her clipboard, campers wrestled their belongings from the carts, and followed their counselors toward the scatter of tattered gray tents, twenty yards to the left of the mess hall.

Okay, Phoebe told herself. Sharing a counselor isn't too bad. Maybe she'll make the six kids she has feel like a family . . . and see that Heather and Tiffany don't do any teasing.

When all the counselors had herded off their charges, Heather and Tiffany, Phoebe and Amy, and two girls who looked about twelve stood unclaimed.

Laurel came striding back, still clutching her clipboard. "Okay. Heather Bowen, Tiffany Reilly, Stephanie Yost, Kelley Gaylord, we're making you . . ." she paused, as if waiting for a drumroll. ". . . Junior Counselors! You'll be in charge of your tent, without any of us in there with you!"

"That means they didn't hire enough counselors this year," Amy whispered to Phoebe.

Tiffany and Heather, Stephanie and Kelley headed for the carts.

Phoebe could feel the muscles at the back of her neck tighten with suspense. Are they putting just those four together? What are they going to do with Amy and me?

Laurel glanced back at the clipboard. "Townsend-Fanchon?"

Phoebe lifted her hand.

Laurel looked up. "Townsend or Fanchon?"

"Both. Or either."

"All right. Fanchon. Bowen's mother insisted we put you in with Reilly and Bowen. Rivas?" Laurel squinted at Amy. "You sure you can handle it, Rivas?"

Amy nodded.

Phoebe walked very slowly toward the carts. I can't go demand to be put in a tent with a counselor, not when Mrs. Bowen told them I was to be with Heather and Tiffany. Besides, that would be like announcing I was afraid of Heather and Tiffany. If *that* got out, I'd be teased worse than I've ever imagined.

The other campers had all gone to their tents when Phoebe and Amy reached the carts. Wondering how to deflect the horse's attention, Phoebe stood back while Amy clambered over the wooden side.

"Hey. Somebody left *suitcases* in here," Amy said.

I could pretend I never saw them before. But that would mean living for two weeks in this same safari outfit, without even a toothbrush. "They're . . . they're mine."

"Oh. Here." Amy handed them down to Phoebe without another word.

This kid has passed up chance after chance to make me feel stupid, Phoebe reflected as they walked toward Tent Nine. The only good thing in this whole day has been meeting Amy Rivas.

Heather and Tiffany, Kelley and Stephanie were rolling out sleeping bags on the cots closest to the front of the tent.

I should have spoken up, Phoebe told herself. I should have said, "Hey, if you're going to throw us in there with Heather and Tiffany, you have to give us a counselor." On the other hand, that Laurel doesn't look like somebody who'd take much from a ten-year-old.

"Oh, *guy!*" Heather glared at Amy. "Now we've practically got a *nursery* school in here!"

"That's it. That's just *it*! I am going to go tell Laurel they have to move those two." Shoving past Amy and Phoebe, Tiffany stormed out of the tent.

Amy dumped her sleeping and duffel bags on the back left cot, and her cowboy boots on the floor.

This kid *hates* being teased, Phoebe marveled, but she's brave enough not to show it here. If a loser like Amy can stand her ground, the least I can do is back her up.

Phoebe dropped her bags with a *thunk* beside Amy's boots.

She was struggling to work the edges of her flowered sheet over the corners of her canvas cot when she realized that everyone in the tent had fallen silent.

"You can't even *talk* to these counselors!" Tiffany stomped back in. "I'm going to have my mother write a letter when we get home." Then she glanced at Heather, who waggled a trembling finger at Phoebe's bedding. "What . . ."

Slapping her hand over her mouth, Tiffany collapsed on her cot, Heather beside her. Kelley and Stephanie hung on to each other, laughing so hard they wheezed.

Phoebe looked down at her cot. There was nothing on it but her sheets.

Quickly, Amy stepped over to help Phoebe smooth them. "Didn't the camp send your parents a list of things for you to bring?"

Phoebe kept her voice low. "I don't know. My parents misplace things a lot."

"That's okay." Amy spread Phoebe's pink blanket over the flowered sheets. "Maybe your mother figured this stuff made more sense than a sleeping bag if you don't go camping a lot."

"I will never go camping again," Phoebe muttered, but only for Amy to hear. "Never. I will shave my head and move into the pantry if my parents ever mention it."

Stepping into the tent, Sumac smiled at Heather. "Over our temper tantrum already, I see. I told you you'd have fun with your tent mates once you got settled."

Tiffany rolled on the cot, gasping.

"Don't get too silly. Lunch is in ten minutes." Sumac walked out, never even glancing at Phoebe.

34

With Sumac gone, Heather and Tiffany, Stephanie and Kelley sat for a minute to recover.

Heather gazed at Phoebe. "Aren't you going to put a ruffled spread over your little pink blankie?"

Tiffany let out a muffled shriek. Kelley and Stephanie shivered with new laughter.

Phoebe shut her suitcase before anyone could glimpse her seersucker spread.

Amy followed her into the sunlight. "You know those guys?"

"Just Heather and Tiffany. We live on the same street."

"*Bummer.*" Amy sat in the dirt, her feet at the edge of the firepit. "There's no point asking to be in a different tent. If that big kid couldn't get us moved, even with a tantrum, it's no use."

Phoebe didn't answer. Two weeks. Two weeks in a place where even your cot has to be dressed like everybody else's. If I can't find a way to get out, if something doesn't *happen* to set me free, the only way I'm going to live through this is to stay out of everybody's way, and be sure nobody notices me. Except for Amy. Without Amy I might not make it here at all.

4

"Hang back a little," Amy advised. "If we're the last ones in to lunch, we can pick a table with kids who don't look as if they'll tease us."

By the time Phoebe and Amy walked into the mess hall, all the other girls were at long steel tables, eating. Phoebe slid her tray down the bars, looking at the row of square, shallow steel pans behind the counter.

As Amy slid her tray along, Cypress, standing behind the counter in a tall chef's hat, waved a ladle at one of the bins. "Casserole?"

Amy hesitated, eyeing the gray, lumpy mixture.

"Okay, stew." Cypress ladled a tan lumpy mix onto Amy's plate. "Rice or potatoes?"

Amy looked at the two bins with white stuff in them. "Which is which?"

"Potatoes," Cypress said, and piled some of the white stuff on Amy's plate.

As Amy moved on, Cypress fixed Phoebe with a flinty gaze.

"I'm a vegetarian," Phoebe said. "My parents sent a note . . ."

"You'll have to take that up with somebody else." Cypress flung casserole and rice onto Phoebe's plate.

Putting a glass of what looked like chocolate milk on her tray, Phoebe followed Amy to a table with five girls who could not have been more than seven years old.

She *is* careful not to be teased, Phoebe marveled.

As she and Amy sat down, the little girls glanced at them briefly, then went on staring at their milk.

Phoebe saw that hers, too, was fading to pale tan as the brown coloring slowly congealed into globs.

"Yummoo," Amy said. "It always does that."

Laurel, near the center of the room, stood up, banging a spoon on a glass. "Listen up, campers! Orientation will be at one thirty today. I want you all lined up outside the mess hall *on the dot!*" She looked down at her clipboard. "Now. Riding schedules, beginning tomorrow: Eight A.M., Wranglers." She read off the names of more than a dozen girls, including Heather and Tiffany. "Nine-thirty, Broncos." She read off more names. "And one P.M., Tenderfeet."

37

Phoebe sat watching her Yummoo coagulate into lumps and sink to the bottom of the glass, until she heard Laurel read her name.

"Hey!" She was so shocked she stood up. "Not me!"

Some of the campers laughed. Some stared at her, appalled.

The laughter faded into uneasy silence as Laurel stared at Phoebe.

"You don't do that." Amy tugged at Phoebe's sleeve, her voice low and solemn. "You don't just stand up and yell at the counselors."

Laurel went on reading off names. Then she announced, "And swimming for everyone at three o'clock. Be sure to bring towels and sunscreen."

Sitting, Phoebe put her elbows on the table, and her forehead in her hands. "Oh, wow."

"You want to go get a piece of carrot cake?" Amy asked.

Phoebe shook her head. "I didn't sign up for horseback riding. And I sure didn't sign up to be shark bait."

"It's not something you sign up for. Everybody does it. Parents figure if their kids don't ride horses and swim at camp, they're not getting their money's worth." As Phoebe started to stand, Amy grabbed her arm. "Don't argue with anybody who's eating this food. They're already in a horrible mood."

As soon as she saw Laurel and the other counselors leave their table, Phoebe went after them. "Excuse me."

Laurel turned. "Not you again."

"Phoebe Townsend-Fanchon. I am not the kind of person who would enjoy riding a horse. I am a city person. I can't think of any time in my whole future when I'll have any need at all to ride a horse."

Laurel looked down at her. "Everybody here rides, unless she's sick."

"As a matter of fact, I get carsick a lot. I could practically guarantee that I'd get horsesick. I wouldn't want to throw up on one of your horses."

"You be at the stables at one tomorrow."

As Laurel stalked away with the other counselors, Amy came out of the mess hall. "I got you a piece of carrot cake," she told Phoebe, "but I ate it. Want to go try to cadge another?"

Phoebe was relieved to see that Tent Nine was empty.

"We ought to change into shorts," Amy advised. "It gets hotter as the day goes on."

"It can't get hotter than this."

"Trust me. It will."

It already felt to Phoebe as if her legs were in khaki chimneys. She took out a pair of the shorts her mother had ordered. They reached almost to Phoebe's knees, like shorts explorers wore in movies about Africa. She had a feeling nobody else would be wearing safari shorts, but the idea of having her legs trapped in long trousers, in the heat, was even more harrowing than being laughed at. Besides, she could stick with Amy on the fringes of the group. And at least the shorts had no pockets over the knees.

The orientation tour started with the bathroom. Some of the campers had changed into shorts. Nobody was wearing shorts that looked remotely like anything one would see on an African explorer. But everyone was watching Laurel.

Standing with the cluster of campers in the concrete-block building, she said, "Notice that the door to the building is propped open with a brick. *That door must be left open at all times!* There's a little problem with the latch, so that it locks if the door closes. And, as you can see, there's only that one tiny window high in the wall, so anybody stuck in here would have no way out."

While Phoebe dreaded attracting attention, the question was so serious she had to know. Let somebody else ask, she begged. Please let somebody else ask.

Nobody else asked.

As Phoebe raised her hand, Laurel looked at her warily.

"What . . . what if you have to go to the bathroom at night?"

The laughter echoed off the walls and stalls.

Phoebe waited until Laurel glared the campers into silence. "I mean, it's at least a block to our tents. Is there any place closer?"

Laurel seemed to be struggling to keep her patience. "This is *it*, Fanchon."

It took all Phoebe's courage to keep talking. "I was just — I was just wondering about stepping on rattlesnakes in the dark."

The campers looked at one another uneasily.

Laurel looked at Sumac.

"Rattlesnakes," Sumac said firmly, "avoid people. Come on."

The campers followed her and Laurel in a straggling line.

"Remember," Sumac cautioned, "whenever you're going from place to place, *stay on the path*. The last thing you want is to spend your time here with poison oak."

She and Laurel marched the campers back past the corral, past the Perrys' house. The ground was hard and rutted, and the sun scorched Phoebe's head, so that she longed to be back in a gentle San Francisco summer drizzle, back where you didn't keep your bathroom door open with a brick, where a person could spend a lifetime without ever coming near a horse or worrying about snakes.

The path widened into a shore, edging the lake. The counselors stopped and the campers flopped down on the bare dirt.

The lake looked even more sinister than it had in the brochure.

"Pond sharks." It slipped out before Phoebe had any idea she was going to say it.

Amy looked stunned. "Pond sharks? You only get sharks in oceans."

The younger campers scooted back from the shore. The older ones looked at Phoebe with even more suspicion and uneasiness than they had in the bathroom. The last thing she wanted to do was attract attention again, but this was a life and death matter. If some poor kid stepped into that lake and anything *gruesome* happened, she would never forgive herself for not bringing it up. "I don't know. They have these fish in South American lakes that can eat — "

"Fanchon, I don't want to hear any more about sharks," Laurel warned.

Amy lifted her hand. "Have there ever been any kids disappearing mysteriously in the water?"

In three long steps, Laurel stood over her. "If you two don't want to be moved to separate tents, you'll cut out this comedy. No one has ever disappeared in our lake. Nobody has ever stepped on a rattler. Come on. Up. Move, everybody."

The other campers took care not to walk close to Phoebe or Amy.

Laurel led the group past the archery range.

I will not ask how many people have been plugged by stray arrows, Phoebe told herself fiercely. Some of these kids are just going to have to speak up for themselves. You can't expect a person in a safari outfit to look out for everybody. She plodded along, feeling a blister growing at the back of her heel.

Beside her, in the weeds, something moved.

"Aaaagh!" Phoebe leaped into the weeds on the other side.

"Stay on the path!" Laurel shrilled.

Campers scattered. Some dashed ahead. Some turned and ran back the other way. But all stayed on the path, except for Phoebe.

"Calm down! Settle down! Stop! Halt! It's nothing!" the counselors yelled.

Even so, it was several minutes before all the campers were collected. They stood, looking ready to bolt at any minute, while Laurel confronted Phoebe.

"We told you never, never to step off the path. Why, Fanchon, why, of all the kids in this camp, did you have to jump into the bushes?"

"Something . . . something moved." Phoebe stood a good distance from where she'd heard the rustling.

"This is the outdoors," Laurel told her grimly. "In the outdoors, things are moving all the time. You have bugs. You have birds. You have toads. You have . . ."

"I thought it might be a snake," Phoebe muttered.

The campers looked at one another anxiously, drawing closer together on the path.

"Believe me, Fanchon," Laurel said, "any snake hearing over fifty people coming is going to head the other way. Snakes do not lie around waiting to be trampled."

She sounded so certain the campers seemed reassured, though not ready to forgive Phoebe. They raked her with looks that would have shriveled a scorpion. They shook their heads. And they walked on, glancing to one side or another a little nervously.

The group passed tent after tent, Laurel explaining what each was for, all the way to Town Hall and back to the mess hall.

I don't care, Phoebe thought. I wouldn't care if they had cable TV in every tent. I just want to take my shoes off and get this dust out of my teeth and not be noticed again until Mrs. Bowen comes back for us.

"You can wash up now," Laurel told the group. "But no wandering around. At five *on the dot* is our big camp cookout! And, *AND*, Cowboy Hank and Lady Lou will be here *in person* to welcome you to Big Tree!"

"How *about* that?" Sumac yelled.

The campers were already straggling off toward the bathroom.

"Want to walk around?" Amy asked.

"What about not wandering?"

"You're allowed to walk. How else would you *get* anyplace? Besides, they just lay all those rules on you the first day to terrorize you so you'll be easy to handle."

There were campers swarming between the tents and the mess hall. A few had recovered enough to scratch hopscotch squares in the dirt.

Heather and Tiffany were standing in a group of older girls.

"It's old Feeble with Rivets!" Heather called.

"Hey, Rivets," Tiffany yelled, "why don't you play hopscotch?"

"Everybody would think it was an earthquake!" Heather shouted.

"No, no, no. An earth*snake*!" Heather chortled.

Amy kept walking. "I'll show you how to put the rest of your stuff away," she told Phoebe. "If you don't have everything just right, the counselors will make you do it over."

A fire was already blazing in the pit when Phoebe and Amy returned.

The campers milled around until Laurel stood and raised her voice. "All right! First we're going to bake potatoes in mud!"

I have had strange meals at home, Phoebe thought, packing mud on her potato. Lunch here was like something off a kindergarten playground. But I *never, never* expected to eat anything this gross. I won't say a word, though. The last thing I need is any more attention.

45

"As soon as your potato is slathered, chuck it into the firepit," Laurel directed.

When all the potatoes had been tossed into the pit, Laurel shoveled hot coals over them.

Phoebe followed the campers who scrambled to rinse their hands under the hose outside the mess hall.

"Hey! Hey! Hey!" Laurel leaped to her feet. "Here they *are!* Our very own Cowboy Hank and Lady Lou Perry are coming to give you a big welcome to Big Tree!"

There was a ragged cheering from the campers.

A green golf cart with a red-and-white striped canvas roof stopped a few yards before the firepit.

Phoebe edged toward the cart. I'll speak right up to the Perrys, she decided. I'll explain there is no reason to take up a horse's time with somebody who doesn't even want to be near it. Anybody who had a kid's television program must understand that not everybody is a horse person. And then I'll bring up the thing about sharks. I can just suggest that a nice picnic at the shore, well back from the water, would be safer than actually going in.

Lady Lou, her outfit so covered with fringe it looked like a colony of octopuses, stepped down from the driver's seat.

Cowboy Hank got out the other side carrying an enormous white cowboy hat.

Phoebe moved closer to them. Right away, Cowboy Hank spotted her. His eyes flickered for a second, as if he'd spied an ambush, and he stepped back slightly.

"Welcome to Camp Big Tree," Lady Lou said, keeping a wary eye on Phoebe.

Easing back, Cowboy Hank waved his hat.

He and Lady Lou climbed back into the golf cart quickly, but not so quickly as if to look alarmed.

As the cart puttered away, Sumac leaped to her feet. "How *about* that!"

The counselors whistled and applauded.

Phoebe was amazed at how alert the Perrys were. Nobody else had noticed her advancing on them, but they had. She stared after the cart. "That's *it*?"

"That's it," Amy said. "And that's all you're going to see of them for the next two weeks."

"They don't associate with us?" Phoebe asked.

"Never," Amy said. "Personally, I get the impression they think of us as another species."

Laurel stood. "Now, campers, we're going to show you how to cook pigs in blankets."

Phoebe whirled. "*Pigs* in *blankets*?" She was too shocked, too outraged, even to think about what anybody thought. "That is horrible! You think I'm going to let you wrap pigs in blankets and *cook* them?"

"Pigs in blankets are just hot dogs in . . ." Amy

47

began, but with everybody around them laughing, Phoebe couldn't hear the rest.

"Quiet! Quiet!" Laurel yelled.

Cypress stepped out of the mess hall and shook her head, lifting her hands, palms up.

"Well, we've got a little problem with our deliveries," Laurel said. "So it's going to be hot dogs on . . ." She squinted at Cypress, who was mouthing words. ". . . on raisin bread. Hey! How's that for something new?"

The campers weren't paying much attention to her. They were still trying to smother their giggles. Every few seconds some of them would glance at Phoebe and collapse into a helpless fit of laughter again.

Besides the sheer humiliation, the idea of pigs cooked in blankets left Phoebe so queasy, she wasn't even tempted to toss a frankfurter on the grill.

She sat with Amy a little to one side, watching campers' hot dogs fall through the grill into the fire, watching the counselors grimly fish them out covered in ashes. If I don't say anything, if I don't even move, she thought, maybe people will overlook me eventually.

Amy claimed her hot dog and wrapped it in a slice of raisin bread. "You sure you don't want — "

"I'm a vegetarian," Phoebe said.

"That's neat." Amy walked to the long picnic

table where the campers clustered looking uncertainly from the mustard to the ketchup, to the relish, to the franks in raisin bread they held in their hands.

"Okay, gang! Come and get 'em," Laurel announced as the counselors began raking potatoes from the pit.

"Hold this and I'll get our potatoes," Amy told Phoebe.

The pickle relish had soaked through the raisin bread. And I was thin before I came here, Phoebe thought bleakly.

The campers attacked their potatoes with grim desperation, hitting them on the ground to crack the mud, chipping away with their fingernails. They were hungry enough now to be serious about their food.

Phoebe scraped her potato with a plastic knife while Amy headed for the hose.

"No washing the mud off!" Laurel yelled. "That's not cookout style! In the true wilderness, you don't have hoses."

Sitting beside Phoebe, Amy tried to stab her potato.

The plastic knife blade snapped off.

"Feeb, no!" Amy warned as Phoebe raised her potato to her face. "You could chip a tooth. Let me grab more raisin bread."

The campers ate in silence, now and then spitting out a bit of ash or mud.

Sumac and Birch eased out of the mess hall carrying a cardboard carton between them.

"*Okay*, guys!" Laurel stood. "Dessert time! We're going to show you how to make *s'mores*! You take marshmallows, and a chocolate bar, and two graham crackers . . ."

Birch whispered something to her. Laurel gazed into the carton.

"Seems somebody forgot to order chocolate and marshmallows," Laurel announced. "So what you do, you put a glob of Yummoo between two graham crackers . . ."

Phoebe ran her tongue around the inside of her mouth. "Yummoo glues itself to your teeth."

"It'd probably be great for anchoring braces," Amy observed. "Grab another graham cracker. It may scrape some off."

"Sing-along time!" Sumac shouted. "Gather 'round, gang!"

The campers clustered closer around the firepit, silent, looking hungry and confused. As the air cooled, tinged with the soft-seeping violet of evening, Phoebe was tempted to ease in closer to the fire. But she was afraid everybody but Amy would move away, or start thinking about her pigs in blankets again.

The counselors took turns singing each song, repeating the words, then urging the campers to sing it.

Phoebe pretended to sing along, in case any-body was watching. She wondered what her grandmother was doing. She wondered whether her parents were thinking about her at all. If they'd had any idea she was going to be forced to ride a horse, would they truly have sent her here?

As the sun sank in a deep red fire, Sumac an-nounced, "We'll have one last song, and then it's lights out."

A sound like some creature in terrible pain came from behind the scrubby trees.

"*Taps*," Amy muttered as Phoebe gasped. "They don't pay the bugler spit."

They waited until everyone else had used the bathroom. "We won't go in until its empty," Amy explained. "The bathroom is where kids really tease you."

Just before lights out, she and Phoebe scurried into Tent Nine. Heather and Tiffany, Kelley and Stephanie were already in their cots.

"Watch out for pigs in the blankets, Feeble," Heather murmured, but the rest were too sleepy to muster more than a few snickers.

Phoebe lay awake long after the others were silent. Her muscles ached, and her legs itched.

What was there to keep rattlesnakes out of the tent? There were no doors or windows to close. A rattlesnake could slither through the camp in the dust at night with nobody to stop it. Or did they have a rattlesnake lookout? The thought was some comfort. She didn't dare ask. From the slow, even breathing in the tent she could tell everybody was asleep. If she woke Amy to ask, and it was a dumb question, she'd never live it down.

She listened to her own breathing. She tried to make it slow and even, hoping that would put her to sleep, half wishing she'd hear a wheeze. With all the dust in Big Tree, she thought, maybe I'll get asthma. Then they'll have to send me home.

But there's nobody there.

She had never felt so alone before.

And she had never itched so.

5

Phoebe was wakened by what sounded like someone who had just gotten heartrending news.

"It's the bugler blowing wake up," Amy muttered drowsily.

Phoebe stayed in her cot until Stephanie and Kelley and Heather and Tiffany left the tent.

Yesterday was the most miserable day of my life, she thought. And today is going to be worse. Today I have to get out of riding a horse and swimming with sharks.

She studied the clothes her mother had packed. She was absolutely certain nobody else would have brought split skirts. Though she was dubious about the Hawaiian print top, it was the only one in the suitcase that didn't look like a safari shirt.

She was suspicous of all her shorts. Her legs itched so that just the thought of covering them hurt, but anything was better than looking totally bizarre.

She settled for a pair of chino slacks.

As she and Amy walked into the mess hall, they were greeted by a few *oinks*, a few pig-and-blanket jokes. As they sat down by the same little girls they'd eaten with the day before, the little girls moved to another table.

Everybody was wearing jeans and plaid or knit shirts. And there's no way to *lose* my clothes, either, Phoebe reflected. Everything I own has my name on it.

She gazed down at the pale grey oatmeal and curled toast before her. "It's going to stay this bad?"

"What?"

"The food."

"Yeah."

"Amy, people *pay* to send their kids here. Some parents even take out loans."

"The parents don't eat here."

"But I'm going to tell mine about this . . . glop."

"Everybody does. But the parents just think their kids are complaining. See, if parents took seriously everything their kids told them, they'd have to *do* something about some of it at least. It's more convenient to think the kids are exaggerating, or just to tune them out. Besides, grown-ups have this firm idea that a summer camp is not supposed to be too comfortable. They think that would make us go soft or something. And Big

Tree is clean, the main cabin looks authentic, there are a lot of things to do, and nobody's ever actually gotten sick from the food, so far as I know."

Laurel stood up. "The activities schedule is posted beside the mess hall door. Read it *the minute* you leave here, and be sure you're signed up for your activities before mail call!"

When Amy and Phoebe approached the list, the other campers sidled away.

Phoebe looked around her. "Amy, listen. We could slip out of here and walk to the nearest town. We could call your folks and tell them they're starving us here."

"You know how far it is to town? It'll be over a hundred degrees by noon. We'd collapse from heatstroke if some motorcycle gang didn't run us down."

"I would risk it." Phoebe rubbed one leg against the other to stop the itching. "I would risk it before I eat any more library paste that they call oatmeal, and before I'd drink any more Yummoo. Amy, think of that stuff sitting in your stomach."

"Come on, Feeb. We have to sign up for things. How about swimming? Oh. Sorry. Archery?"

"If I got shot in the foot with an arrow, could they still force me to climb on a horse? They sure couldn't make me go in the water with a bandage on."

Amy was solemn. "You have to have a lot of

practice before you can shoot yourself in your own foot. And if you think I'm going to do it for you, forget it. It turns my stomach just to dig a *sliver* out. Meanwhile, if we keep standing here, Laurel's going to come back and pick an activity for us."

Phoebe could imagine Laurel forcing her to hike through snake-infested underbrush. "Okay. Arts and crafts. Maybe I'll step on a needle so I can't put my foot in the footholder."

"Stirrup."

"Or walk on the beach."

"Feeb, only nerds go *near* the craft tent."

"Sounds good to me."

The craft tent was a jumble of easels, tables, jars of paint, brushes, yarn, wood, and junk that seemed to Phoebe to have no possible use.

On a folding chair next to a wooden carton, Cypress sat reading *People*.

"No." She didn't look up. "No, you can not borrow my yarn to replace a broken shoelace. No, I will not sew up your torn jeans. No, I do not have anything you can use to make a fishing pole."

"We were thinking about doing arts and crafts," Amy told her.

Cypress dropped her magazine on the carton. "You're kidding. Nobody ever comes in here to do crafts!" She led them around the clutter in the tent. "How about making lanterns from tin cans?

Belts! Did you ever make a belt? Wait. I've got it. Macramé!" She began sorting out a tangle of cord.

It was peaceful in the tent, sorting and tying cords, Cypress turning pages.

We should have picked a noisy activity, with a lot of confusion to take my mind off horses and sharks and this itch on my legs, Phoebe thought. Fleas. The tent must be full of fleas. The *camp* must be full of fleas. But according to Amy, parents expect their kids to put up with all this misery.

Phoebe tied.

"When our folks ask 'What did you do at camp?' we can say 'Knotting,'" Amy murmured. "And they'll say, 'We spent a fortune to send you there to do nothing?'"

Phoebe didn't look up from her cords.

"Knotting, nothing. Get it?"

Phoebe nodded, but even a real joke wouldn't have gotten her mind off the fact she was going to be face-to-face with a horse in a few hours, then a shark-infested lake, if the itching on her legs didn't send her screaming from this camp.

Amy shook her head. "It's amazing the money parents spend to make their kids miserable."

Cypress looked at her watch. "Mail call."

"Why don't I just stay here and work on my macramé," Phoebe said. "I don't mind skipping lunch. I don't even mind missing horseback riding, or swimming."

"Go." Cypress went back to her magazine.

"I wouldn't be getting mail this soon."

Amy stood. "If your parents feel *really* guilty about making you come, they might have sent a package right off, yesterday, by overnight express. Mine did, the first year they sent me."

Phoebe was not convinced. Her parents hadn't shown any serious guilt at all.

"Out," Cypress commanded.

Pine and Oak stood on Town Hall's porch distributing letters and parcels.

All the letters were claimed, and most of the packages, when Oak picked up a large box. "Fanchon!"

"That's you! That's you!" Amy urged Phoebe forward.

Heather and Tiffany followed them back to Tent Nine, along with Kelley and Stephanie and two girls Phoebe didn't even know.

It felt almost like being popular. At the same time, it was sad. Except for Amy, none of these kids would be caught dead hanging out with me, Phoebe realized. And all it takes is a box that might have food in it to make them follow me like . . . like friends. And whatever it is, I'll share it.

She stopped to scratch the back of her right leg

with the toe of her left shoe. All of the girls walking with her stopped.

Knowing what these kids have been living on, how could I open a box of treats and eat in front of them? Phoebe reasoned. Besides, if I share, they may decide that I'm basically okay. They might back me up when I tell Laurel I will not ride a horse. They might even respect me for standing up for myself.

"It's so heavy." She set the box on her cot and scratched through her chinos.

"Boy." Amy sounded awed. "We are talking real guilt!" She sat on the cot beside Phoebe. "I shouldn't even stick around. But I'll go light on Macaroni Surprise at dinner."

"Pound cake. What do you want to bet there's a pound cake?" Tiffany plopped down on the other side of Phoebe.

"And tortilla chips!" One of the strange girls squatted beside the cot. "With those big bags of popcorn!"

"Homemade fudge. With nuts," Heather declared. "And maybe English toffee!"

Phoebe scratched both legs through her slacks, then pulled the first package out of the newspaper crushed in the box.

Amy squinted at it. "*Figs*?"

"Figs in blankets," Heather muttered, but everybody except Phoebe looked at her coldly.

"Prunes." Phoebe took out another bag.

"Pine nuts." Amy's voice was flat. "Raw pine nuts."

"What's that plastic bottle?" Heather demanded.

Phoebe lifted it out of the box and looked at the label. "Soy protein wafers."

"Wouldn't you know?" Heather muttered in disgust. "Wouldn't you just *know*?"

From the carton, Phoebe took a bottle of vitamin C tablets, a box of menthol-eucalyptus throat lozenges, and a can of mosquito repellant. She fished through the papers, but there was nothing else. Nothing to eat. Nothing to put on an itch.

"Honest to Pete!" Getting to her feet, Tiffany stalked out of the tent with Heather and Stephanie and Kelley and the strange girls.

"What do you expect from a kid that wears saddle shoes to camp?" Kelley demanded.

Amy put her arm around Phoebe's shoulder. "Your parents must be very interesting people."

"How many parents manage to humiliate their own kids even by *mail*?" Even saying that much made Phoebe uneasy. She loved Iris and Brian, she knew they loved her, and she was scared to realize that at this moment she resented them. She looked at the bottle of throat lozenges. "If I ate all these, do you think I'd throw up? They wouldn't make anybody who was throwing up ride a horse."

"Feeb, let's go eat."

Phoebe felt a kind of dark and reckless despair. "Why not? With any luck, I'll get food poisoning. But it's got to set in before one."

Sitting with Amy alone at the long table, Phoebe peeled back the top slice of bread and peered at the sandwich filling. "What do you think it is?"

Amy looked closely at her own sandwich filling. "Um . . . I think maybe we should stick with those protein wafers your folks sent."

Phoebe was itching too badly to care about food, anyway. She sat scratching her left ankle with the heel of her right foot. *Here I worried about horses and sharks and snakes, and I never gave a thought to fleas.*

She waited until Laurel and the other counselors stood. "It's now or never. I've got to tell her I'm not riding any horse."

"It won't do any good." But Amy followed.

Phoebe caught up with Laurel outside the mess hall. "Excuse me." The other campers stood at a safe distance, watching.

If I can convince her it would be genuine cruelty to make a person itching the way I do ride a horse . . . no. No, that will only make everybody tease me more. Or they'll pretend to be afraid of catching fleas from me. I'll ask to speak to her privately.

61

Laurel turned. "No. Whatever it is, no."

Walking back to Tent Nine, Phoebe could feel her mouth get dry and her hands get cold. "What would they do if I just didn't show up at the corral?"

"They'd hunt you down like a dog," Amy said.

"That's not funny, Amy."

The tent was empty.

"Feeb, you're getting kind of a . . . kind of a reputation around here. I don't think you want to make it any worse." Amy peeled off her shorts and struggled into jeans.

That must be what she's going to wear riding, Phoebe realized. Her parents must not have had enough money to buy her jodhpurs.

Phoebe got her riding britches out of her big suitcase. Oh, boy, are they going to itch me, she thought miserably. She took off her chinos — and she saw her legs.

She went all quivery and weak inside. Fleas! Of course! She was almost certain that it was fleas that spread bubonic plague, the Black Death that wiped out half of Europe in the Middle Ages.

"Amy . . ."

Amy was pulling her pointy-toed boots on.

"Amy, what do you know about the Black Death, the plague that wiped out . . ."

"Oh, come on, Feeb." Amy sounded almost exasperated. "Just ride the dumb horse." Then she looked at Phoebe. "Oh, wow. Your legs!"

"Better stay clear of me." Phoebe could hear her voice go tight and dry. "Just go have somebody call my folks."

"For poison oak?"

It took a second for the relief to sink in. "Poison . . . poison oak?" Dreadful as it sounded, Phoebe knew it was nothing compared to the plague.

Amy was calm. "Sure. That's why they yell at you not to wander into the bushes. We've got poison oak all over the hills behind my house, too. I've had it a couple of times. It's miserable, but nothing to call home about. I'll go get Laurel. You don't want to spread it."

"Spread it? Amy, you think I've already given it to . . ."

"Nah. Not to anybody else. You don't want to spread it all over yourself."

Phoebe sat in her underwear staring at her legs. They looked horrible, covered with tiny red weepy blisters. While it was an enormous relief not to have bubonic plague, she could not help reflecting that her parents had sent her off to suffer even more than she'd dreamed she would.

Amy was back with Laurel in minutes. Laurel squatted and gazed at Phoebe's legs. "See? See? *That's* why we told you to stay out of the bushes. Okay, put your shorts on. You don't want cloth over that mess. Rivas, you go ahead to the stables."

Cypress was in the craft tent, alone, reading a Harlequin Romance paperback, when Laurel herded Phoebe in.

"Poison oak." Laurel steered Phoebe over to Cypress.

"Oh, boy." Setting down the book, Cypress peered at Phoebe's legs. "Turn around."

Phoebe turned.

"The backs, too." Cypress sighed.

It occurred to Phoebe that maybe poison oak could be right up there with the plague, if you got a bad enough case. "Am I going to . . ."

Cypress stood. "You're going to be fine. But you should have told somebody before it spread like that. How in the world did you manage to get in poison oak? You're the first kid to get it in all the years I've been here."

She didn't really seem to expect an answer, and Phoebe was not eager to recount the humiliation of leaping into the bushes.

"I'll see you after riding, Fanchon," Laurel said, and left.

After riding! The relief that flooded over Phoebe almost made the itching worthwhile. She had no idea how bad this poison oak was going to get. Right now, wretched as it felt, it was easier to bear than the idea of sitting on a horse.

"Come on. I'll take you to the infirmary." Cypress put the Harlequin Romance in the pocket of her shirt.

Infirmary! Feeling all shaky again, Phoebe followed Cypress. *They act so casual about my poison oak, but if that's all it is, would they put me in the infirmary? Maybe they just don't want to alarm me. Maybe they don't want to give me the true diagnosis until they've done a lot of tests. Blood tests. What if they plan to take a bunch of blood out of my arm? I will tell them they're not getting a drop until they call my parents.*

She trudged after Cypress into Town Hall, through the big front room into a room that was not at all authentic. It had recessed ceiling lights, and three cots with white sheets and army blankets. In the center of the room was a steel table, with a roll of butcher paper at its head. Against one wall were banks of cupboards, a stainless steel sink, and shelves with bottles and boxes.

"That looks like an autopsy table." It had to be said.

Cypress glanced at her and for a second seemed to smile. "Nothing that interesting. Hop up there."

There is obviously no reason why there'd be an autopsy table at a summer camp, Phoebe told herself firmly. If they lost so many kids they needed an autopsy table, word would surely get around, and nobody would send their kids. Not even parents going on a concert tour.

She lay on the table while Cypress slathered

thick pink lotion on her legs. It felt clammy, but in a moment the itching eased.

Cypress tore off a long piece of butcher paper and spread it over the third cot. Then she took the pillows off two of them and plumped them atop the pillow on the third.

"You can lie here, but keep your knees bent so your legs dry."

Riding time must have started. Phoebe took off her shoes. *With any luck my legs won't dry until it's over! I won't say a word. If Laurel asks why I didn't show up, I only have to tell her I was kept in the* infirmary. *You can't argue with that.*

Cypress arranged the pillows so that Phoebe could sit up on the cot, legs bent, and then left the room.

Are they just going to abandon me here? Phoebe wondered.

Cypress came back with a dozen ancient, dog-eared comic books. "Here you go. Take it easy."

Little Lulu, Archie, Donald Duck, Marvel Comics . . . Phoebe's parents had never bought her a comic book. They bought her fine hardcover books — *The Bat Poet,* all the Pooh books, Dr. Seuss.

She lay back against the pillows, knees bent, reveling in the sheer tackiness of reading comic books.

Now this, she thought, *this would be a tolerable way to spend two weeks at camp.*

Cypress wandered back in. "Want a Popsicle?"

"Oh, sure!"

Phoebe licked the purple juice beginning to ooze off the Popsicle. For the first time since she'd arrived at Big Tree, she felt at peace.

She had finished the comic books and was feeling pleasantly drowsy, when Cypress reappeared.

"Swim time."

Phoebe sat up straight. *"What?"*

"Time to suit up for swimming."

"Me? I can't go swimming! Look at my legs!"

Cypress filled a pint-size bottle with pink lotion from an enormous container on top of a counter.

"I'll contaminate the whole pond with poison oak!"

"I don't want you to go in. But you have to show up at the lake."

"But I'm all covered in dry *goop*."

Cypress was unmoved. "Your parents are paying for you to go to camp, not lie around an infirmary, reading comic books." She handed Phoebe the pint of lotion. "You stay out of the water, and sit on a towel. Use your sunscreen on the rest of you, but keep your legs well-covered with lotion. I'll want to check on you every few hours until it's all cleared."

There is a point where you know it is absolutely no use in arguing with an adult.

This, Phoebe could tell, was the point.

She walked back to Tent Nine, keeping her gaze

fixed on the ground so she wouldn't have to meet the eyes of the few stragglers on the path.

Stay inconspicuous, she thought. That was what I was going to do. And here I am walking along like a pale, pink-frosted gingerbread nerd. What a field day Heather and Tiffany and Stephanie and Kelley will have when I show up at the lake.

I could refuse. I could just stay in the tent.

And that Cypress would probably come haul me out. That Cypress is *fierce*.

Amy was waiting in the tent, wearing a navy blue one-piece bathing suit. "Better hurry," she advised. "You get in trouble if you don't show up where you're supposed to be."

"Look at me." Phoebe knew she sounded overly dramatic, but she was too despondent to care.

"Look at me. How would you like to be this stocky in a bathing suit? Nobody's going to notice how kids our age look."

Sumac stepped into the tent. "Come on, you two."

"I can't swim," Phoebe announced. There was no harm trying. "All the lotion would wash off."

"I know. You can sit on the shore. Bring a towel."

Amy was right. Nobody noticed her, or Phoebe. The campers were standing on the shore, at the edge of the water, motionless, while Laurel ranted at them.

68

Seeing Phoebe, Laurel called, "You! Over here!"

Is she going to keep at me about the poison oak? Phoebe wondered. But from her voice, I'd better get over there fast.

"Look!" Laurel greeted her.

Phoebe gazed down at her coated legs.

"No, no, no!" Laurel gestured toward the campers, who stood silent, looking stubborn but somehow anxious. *Tell them.*

"Pardon?"

Staring at Phoebe's frosted legs, some of the campers edged away from her, but no closer to the lake.

"One kid." Laurel shook her head. "One kid, and you've demoralized this whole camp. You've got kids afraid to go to the bathroom in the dark. Now you're going to have them worrying about poison oak. But this . . . swimming is supposed to be one of the best parts of camping. Swimming is fun! Swimming is healthful! Swimming is why we have this lake! And thanks to your talk about sharks, nobody will set a *toe* in the water. I want you to explain to everyone, right now, that there are no such things as pond sharks, that you made up the whole story."

"I . . ."

Laurel narrowed her eyes. "You made it up. Tell them."

No, Phoebe thought. No. She won't bully me

into confessing to something that's not true.

"Fanchon . . ." Laurel warned.

"She meant pool sharks," Amy said suddenly.

Phoebe stared at her, astonished.

Even Laurel seemed taken aback. *"Pool sharks?"*

Amy nodded. "She was thinking of pool sharks, people who go to pool halls and pretend not to know the game. Hotshot players challenge them to play for money, and then the pool sharks win."

Laurel seemed to consider this for a second. "Pool sharks. *Pool* sharks!" She turned to the campers ringing the lake. "See? Now, I don't want any more nonsense from anybody about sharks!"

Not a camper moved. Not a camper spoke.

"Rivas just explained!" Laurel seemed almost to beseech the campers. *"There are no such things as pond sharks!* Now, everybody in!"

The campers stood looking at her, uneasy but unmoved.

Stepping to Laurel's side, Sumac whispered in her ear.

"What do you mean, control myself?" Laurel exploded. She leveled a finger at Phoebe. "You. Out of my sight." She turned to Sumac. "Take her away from here."

"I'll walk her back to our tent," Amy volunteered.

"Fine. Good. Just *get her out of my face!*"

Laurel seemed dangerously close to losing her composure entirely.

Phoebe and Amy walked back to the tent silently.

I disgraced myself again, Phoebe thought miserably.

And there was an even more urgent matter to consider. *"Pool sharks?"* she asked.

"I've been thinking about it," Amy said. "I figured that's what you must have meant. Everybody's heard of pool sharks. Nobody's heard of pond sharks."

This sounded terribly, terribly sensible to Phoebe. "You think so?" she asked cautiously.

"Sure."

"You mean I scared over fifty people about something that doesn't even *exist?*"

"Scared yourself, too. Besides, this is a manmade lake, dug right out of the ground. They'd have to truck in sharks."

Phoebe sat on her cot, stricken. "I bet nobody at this camp has ever made such a fool of herself."

The rash lasted four days. For four days, Phoebe tried. She tried to play volleyball. "I have never," Sumac said solemnly on the fourth day, "seen one kid manage to hit the ball so many times with her head and not once with her hands."

She tried to go on hikes. She stayed on the path.

"Poison oak and blisters." Cypress finished

71

bandaging under Phoebe's ankle bone. "You're a whole medical emergency, all by yourself. Didn't anybody ever tell you you can't hike in saddle shoes?"

She did not go near the lake. Laurel forbade it. Laurel had persuaded most of the campers that Phoebe meant pool sharks, but a few of the younger ones couldn't be convinced there could not be sharks in swimming pools.

She even tried to eat the food.

The craft tent was her refuge. She and Amy worked tirelessly on their macramé creations.

Day after day, Cypress watched the work grow. Finally, she asked, "Um . . . what are you guys making?"

"Macramé," Amy said.

"Very impressive. Could you just give me an idea what they are?"

"They are large." Phoebe went on tying.

On the fifth day, Laurel was waiting for her, outside the mess hall, after lunch. "See you at the corral at one-thirty, Fanchon."

Phoebe was shocked. She hadn't thought about horses for days. "I don't want to stir up my rash."

"You're all cleared up."

Laurel strode away.

Walking back to Tent Nine with Amy, Phoebe tried to think of another reason not to ride. But who would take seriously a kid who believed in pond sharks?

"What if I go to the infirmary and tell Cypress I have a stomachache? No. Cypress is tougher than Laurel."

Amy didn't even change jeans. Poor kid, Phoebe thought. If her parents have enough money to send her here, they should at least buy her the right kind of riding britches. "I could step into poison oak again. Nah. They'd know I did it on purpose."

Amy was putting on her pointy-toed boots. It's really sad, Phoebe thought. She doesn't even have a pair of real riding boots. "All right. I'll just go to the corral and announce that I am not going to ride, that I have a right to refuse. Everybody treats me like a joke around here, but when they see me stand up to Laurel, they'll have to respect me."

Phoebe got her jodhpurs out. I should be grateful that my mother has been to horse shows. I may not talk right or act right, I may even get weird food packages, I may have a lot of trouble refusing to ride a horse, but at least I'll look classy when I do it.

Still, she thought, if I had jeans, I'd wear them so Amy wouldn't feel so embarrassed. At least I won't make her feel any more tacky by wearing my wool jacket. It'd probably suffocate me in this heat, anyway. I'll settle for my white turtleneck shirt, since I'm not actually going to ride anyway.

Phoebe sat on her cot and worked her legs into the jodhpurs.

Getting into her boots took Phoebe even more time than putting on the jodhpurs. What a lot of fuss, she thought, to get ready not to ride a horse. But they'll know it's not just because I don't have the right clothes for it.

Finally, she stood.

Amy was looking at her. "That's what you're going to wear?"

Phoebe nodded. "My mother has seen a lot of horse shows."

"I was just asking," Amy said.

There were few campers out in the searing heat. Those they passed stared at them, then tittered, or laughed outright.

Dumb kids, Phoebe thought disgustedly, making fun of Amy just because she doesn't have the right kind of boots and riding britches. To get Amy's mind off having the wrong clothes, she asked, "Do horses eat pine nuts?"

"I don't know. There are some crazy horses."

"I brought some. I'm going to explain to Laurel that I'm absolutely not going to ride. But if a horse gets near me in the meantime, I want to throw it something horses like. That way, at least it won't rear up at me."

"Feeb, you don't *throw* treats at a horse."

"Amy, *I* do."

Heather and Tiffany were sitting on the corral fence.

Tiffany looked at Phoebe, shrieked, then clapped her hand over her mouth.

Phoebe went on talking to Amy. "I'm going to say, 'Look, Laurel, I'm a city person. I can tell you most of the stores in downtown San Francisco. I know my way around the Palace of Fine Arts and the De Young Museum. I know where the best mimes hang out at Ghirardelli Square, and the easiest place to get on a cable car. I know about everything I need to know to get around in the city.'"

Heather slid off the fence and sat in the dirt, laughing so hard tears ran down her cheeks.

I have had it with them, Phoebe thought suddenly. She stopped. "Okay, you guys. So there are no pond sharks. Big deal."

"Ignore them." Taking Phoebe by the arm, Amy pushed open the corral gate.

Sumac, Birch, and Laurel stood by the stable in jeans and plaid shirts and cowboy boots. None of the little girls with them looked older than seven or eight, but they all wore cowboy boots and jeans and knit or plaid shirts. Nobody wore riding britches or round-toed boots or turtlenecks.

Sumac, standing beside Laurel, looked at Phoebe and then turned away quickly. Birch punched Sumac's arm, but her own face was pink and she bit her lower lip.

For all the dreadful afternoon heat, Phoebe felt suddenly clammy. *My mother has been to horse shows — but she has never been to camp.*

It was plainly an effort for Laurel to keep her face solemn, but she managed to glare at Heather and Tiffany. "Okay, you two! No hanging around the corral when you're not riding! And you, Rivas and Fanchon, get over here."

Cackling, Heather and Tiffany staggered away.

Birch and Sumac walked into the stable. It seemed to Phoebe she could hear their muffled laughter.

Phoebe felt sick and dizzy. *I could walk out of here, but they'd bring me back. They'd bring me back in my round-toed boots and jodhpurs, in front of the whole camp.*

Laurel glanced at Phoebe again, then down at the ground. Finally she took a deep breath, and looked up, careful not to let her eyes stray toward Phoebe's boots or shirt or britches. "All right, Tenderfeet. We're going to show you how to mount and dismount and make your horse do what you want." She stepped over to a sleek, black horse Birch led out of the stable. "Okay, Siren."

Laurel got on and off the horse, and showed how she did not hold on to the saddle, and how to work the reins.

Phoebe barely noticed. *Standing here in this*

outfit is punishment enough for everything I ever did wrong in my life — and anything wrong I will ever do, she thought. There's no need to make me sit on a horse, too.

Heatstroke. If I stand perfectly still in this horrible heat, I may just drop in the dust. They'd have to carry me back to the tent in front of everybody in these clothes, but I wouldn't know. I'd be unconscious. I don't care if the tent is like an oven, so long as I can stay in there with nobody to see me, except maybe Amy.

Laurel nodded at one of the little girls. "Now, let's get you up on Lollipop."

With a boost from Birch, the little girl scrambled onto the mottled gray mare Sumac had brought out.

If I'm going to keel over, Phoebe thought, it had better be now.

As more horses were led from the stable and more Tenderfeet seated, Phoebe was careful not to make eye contact with any of the horses. If it's true they can sense fear, I'm giving off enough to stampede the whole pack . . . bunch . . . herd.

"Okay, Rivas," Laurel said. "Take Sugar."

Amy stepped right up to a tawny horse and got herself onto his back with no help.

"We'll put Fanchon on Flash," Laurel said.

Sumac walked into the stable.

Flash? Phoebe felt her turtleneck tighten around her windpipe. *What are they doing putting a kid my age on an animal named Flash?*

It's this outfit! It may look hilarious, but it must make Laurel think I've been in a lot of horse shows!

The girls already on mounts, sat looking only a little nervous. The horses didn't snort, or try to bite.

But none of them was named Flash.

It's too late to reason with these people. The only thing to do is get out of here without setting off a horse riot.

As Phoebe backed slowly toward the gate, Sumac strode out of the stable, leading the most ancient animal Phoebe had ever seen. Its coat was a dull patchy brown, its mane was thin and scraggly, and all its ribs showed. It walked with its head down, as if each step took great, great thought and effort.

"Here you go," Sumac said.

Phoebe stepped back again. "Here I go what?"

"Up on Flash."

"*Flash?*"

The beast didn't even lift its head.

Laurel, on Siren, urged, "Come on, Fanchon. The hour is passing."

Phoebe had never thought to meet a horse so piteous it needed her protection. "That Flash is too old to carry *anybody*! The poor old thing should be in her stable lying down."

"You're going to ride her if we have to hold you on." Laurels' voice was cool and firm.

They might just do it, Phoebe thought. If there's anything worse than riding a horse, it's being held on a horse. Imagine all these little kids each on her own horse, and some counselor holding me on Flash.

There was no hope. There was no way out. It was too late for a sunstroke. "Okay. Okay. Just don't rush me."

Sumac made a basket of her hands and held them down by Flash's side. "Step up," she told Phoebe.

"On your *hands*?"

"Do it!" Laurel ordered.

Phoebe stepped on Sumac's hands, bent her knees, and sprang up.

Even as Phoebe landed in the dirt beside her, Flash did not move.

"No! No! No!" Laurel groaned. "You put your leg *over* the horse."

Sumac and Birch hauled Phoebe to her feet and boosted her into the saddle, shoved her feet into the stirrups, and slapped the reins into her hand, while all the Tenderfeet except Amy giggled.

Carsick is nothing. Phoebe watched Sumac and Birch mount the last two horses We haven't *moved* and already I feel horsesick.

As Laurel rode Siren out of the corral, the other

horses followed as if attached by a string.

Except for Flash. Flash stood studying her front hooves.

Sumac rode up beside Phoebe. "Kick her."

"Pardon?"

"Kick her!" Birch, on the other side, repeated.

"I'm not going to kick a poor old horse that's just standing here resting!"

Sumac smacked Flash on the neck.

Flash lifted her head.

With Phoebe holding on desperately to the saddle horn, Flash turned and walked into the stable.

"Fanchon, you get on out here!" Birch bellowed.

As Flash ambled toward a stall, Sumac came riding in.

"This horse knows pretty much what she wants to do," Phoebe told her, but Sumac grabbed the reins and led Flash from the stable into line behind the last Tenderfoot. "Shape up!" she snapped, prying Phoebe's hands off the saddle horn and handing her the reins.

Laurel led the string of horses west, away from the tents and buildings. Birch rode along beside the line, and Sumac stayed behind Flash.

The sun seared Phoebe's hair, and the dust stirred up by the horses ahead sifted into her nose.

"Kick her!" Sumac slapped Flash to keep her moving. "And let go of that saddle horn, Fanchon!"

I am not going to kick anything that could get

my whole leg in her teeth. Phoebe hung on to the horn. And I'm not going to let go of the only thing that's keeping me on this saddle. Fall off in this wilderness and you'll probably land in a nest of rattlesnakes. And if Sumac smacks this old horse one more time, I'm turning the whole camp in to the SPCA.

Flash plodded on. She was so deliberate, and so slow, that Phoebe almost began to relax. This was not a bad old horse, Phoebe thought.

Even the dust seemed to settle as they rode along. On either side of the trail, now, were scrubby gray-green bushes. Over the plonk-plonk-plonk of hooves, Phoebe thought she heard the sound of running water.

A minute later she saw a narrow brook running over smooth, shiny gray rocks.

As the horses ahead of her crossed the stream, Flash stopped.

"Oh, come on!" Phoebe remonstrated. "It barely covers your feet!"

Flash stepped into the water.

Suddenly, to her astonishment, Phoebe found herself pitching forward. She clutched the horn harder to keep from sliding right down the horse's neck.

"Fanchon! Get off! Jump!"

Sumac sounded so scared that Phoebe scrambled off Flash's back without even thinking about how to do it.

Kneeling in the water, Flash gave a great snort and rolled onto her side. If it weren't for the saddle, Phoebe saw, the horse would have rolled on her back like a puppy.

"I never saw her do a thing like that before! Never!" Laurel came riding back to them. "Are you all right, Fanchon?"

Phoebe got to her feet, her riding pants soaking, cold water in her boots.

"Don't you know you could have been rolled on?" Laurel sounded shaken. "Why didn't you pull her up?"

"Pull her *up*?" Phoebe looked at Flash, who was clambering to her feet. "Do you know how much that horse must weigh?"

"No, no, no, no!" Laurel cried. "Pull up on the *reins*. Didn't you listen to a word I said at the corral?"

Phoebe could see all the Tenderfeet watching, big-eyed.

"I am finished with riding today. I am finished with riding altogether." Even to herself, Phoebe sounded firm and dignified. Turning, she walked stiffly away. She walked a good two or three minutes before she ran.

The sun was hot on her back, but her pants stuck clammy and cold to her legs, and her boots squished, as she strode up the long walk to the Perrys' house. She tried to make herself look like a person full of purpose and dignity.

The sprinklers sent a fine mist over her. Two men trimming the bushes glanced up for a second, but neither spoke.

The heavy, horseshoe-shaped knocker fell on the door with a great resounding *thooonk*.

For a second, Phoebe didn't recognize the woman who opened the door.

Lady Lou wore a shiny blue kimono, the kind displayed in the windows at the touristy souvenir shops all over Chinatown, kimonos that usually had embroidered dragons on the back. She was barefoot, and her feet had bunions. All of her luxuriant yellow curls were gone, along with her blue eyeshadow. Her hair was short and brown, frizzy and skimpy. She stared at Phoebe, astonished, apprehensive.

"Excuse me . . . ," Phoebe began.

Lady Lou looked even more alarmed to hear words come from a camper. "Henry!" she cried.

"What is it?" came a voice from another room.

"It's . . . it's one of *them*!"

Cowboy Hank Perry came padding into the room, wearing an old brown bathrobe and brown felt slippers and carrying a can of cola.

". . . One of the girls," Lady Lou finished.

Cowboy Hank seemed as astounded as his wife to see a camper at the door.

Phoebe gathered all her courage. "The thing is

this. I can't stay here any longer. . . ." She talked on and on. She explained about her parents' tour, about the poison oak, about Flash trying to roll her into river gravel. She even brought up her grandmother on vacation.

Neither Perry said a word. They stared at her, stunned by this breach of everything they held right and proper.

Finally, when she could think of nothing more to say, Phoebe drew a deep breath.

"You . . . you go along, now," Lady Lou said, as if trying to placate a threatening dog. "You go on back to your riding class."

"Lesson," Cowboy Hank said.

"It's not a *lesson*," Lady Lou murmured.

"Well, it's not a class, either."

Lady Lou looked down at Phoebe. "You go on . . . you go to wherever you're supposed to be now."

Soggy and panting, Phoebe tromped up the steps of Town Hall.

Cypress sat on the porch, crossing off entries on a menu. "Closed," she said as Phoebe reached for the door.

"I have to locate my parents. I am leaving here."

"A lot of newcomers have a bad time at first. In a few days, you'll adjust."

"I am sure I will not. Whatever it takes, I am getting out of here."

"No," Cypress said.

"You think you can force me to stay?"

"You've got no place else to go, kid," Cypress said. "Why don't you get out of those crazy boots and britches, and go swim or something."

6

As Phoebe trudged away from Town Hall, she saw Amy heading toward her.

"I've been looking everyplace for you!" Amy said. "You'd better come back to the tent and change."

"Is anybody in there?"

"In this heat? Everybody's down at the lake."

In the tent, Phoebe pulled off her boots and changed into dry clothes. "I was almost starting to like that horse."

"She didn't mean anything by it. She just suddenly felt good. It wouldn't happen again in a million years."

"Right. And it picked me to happen to." Phoebe stuffed protein tablets into her shirt pockets. "I'm not waiting around here for the next once in a million . . ." She stopped as Laurel strode into the tent.

"You don't just walk away from a riding session, Fanchon. When you have trouble with a horse, you have to face it right away. Otherwise, you'll never get the nerve to ride again."

"Fine. Great. I will never have the nerve to ride again."

"*Up.*"

"My throat's all raw. I think I'm coming down with something."

"Now."

Amy handed Phoebe the bag of throat lozenges. "I might as well come, too."

"No," Laurel told her. "This is something Fanchon has to do herself."

"I can at least stand by." Amy was firm.

"Don't make trouble, Rivas," Laurel said sternly.

"Trouble? Trouble?" Phoebe looked at Laurel straight on. "You are a bully, and this whole camp is dumb."

"And Cowboy Hank sings like a mule with the croup," Amy added.

"Fanchon, put on your shoes. Rivas, you just elected yourself to clean the bathroom. Cypress will give you what you need."

Even with Laurel coaching her, Phoebe fumbled with the cinch strap, but at last she got it undone.

If this were a movie, Phoebe thought, I could blind her momentarily with a shovelful of manure and make a dash for it.

This is no movie.

And there's a whole corral full of horses out there.

"Laurel!" somebody yelled from a distance. "Phone call!"

Laurel hung Flash's saddle on a wall peg. "Practice a few times with the cinch off the horse," she told Phoebe and hurried out of the stable.

Phoebe stood for a moment in the dimness before she realized she was alone with Flash, and with more horses outside. *Don't call for help.* That would be tacky . . . and it might bring the horses running. Laurel said to be at dinner by five! What if the horses eat earlier? What if they come in here to wait for dinner, and there's only me, cornered?

"Just stay calm," she murmued to Flash. "And if you guys have ESP, tell that gang outside to take it easy, too."

This is the bravest thing I have ever done in my life, and I'm only doing it because I'm more scared of being trapped in the stable by a herd of beasts. Phoebe made herself walk slowly across the corral. I should whistle casually to reassure them, if I could get up enough spit. Nah, they'd know I was faking. She kept her eyes on the corral gate, not even glancing toward the horses, but hearing every *clop-clop-clop* as they moved around.

Once out the gate, she resisted the terrible urge to run. They could jump the fence in a second and gallop right over me, she reminded herself. She walked on, barely daring to blink, still hearing the *clop-clop-clop* of hooves.

I will hear those hooves in my head as long as I live, she thought. It's as if they're right behind me even now. Once I get to the bathroom, I'll dunk my head in cold water and sit down until I get the sound of hooves out of my skull.

As she came around a bend in the path, she saw Heather and Tiffany coming out of the bathroom.

"Hey, Feeble! I hear you got dumped in the stream! I hear . . ." Tiffany stared past Phoebe. "Oh, wow! What are you doing with the horse?"

Clop . . . clop . . . clop. Phoebe felt hot, wet breath on the back of her head.

As she bolted past them into the bathroom, Heather and Tiffany leaped aside.

Clop-clop-clop.

Phoebe turned, her back to the window wall. "Oh, no! Shoo! Go home, Flash!" As she edged along the wall, the horse plodding toward her, she saw a sneaker-clad foot kick the brick away from the door.

The door slammed shut.

Phoebe pressed her back against the wall.
Clop-clop . . .
She looked up at the horse's enormous wet nose.

Don't make her nervous! She could squash you into the floor in a second.

"Here! Here!" Phoebe pulled a throat lozenge from her pocket.

Closing her eyes, she held the lozenge out on the palm of her hand. *Better she bites my fingers off than tramples me into mush.*

Phoebe felt soft, wet, slobbery lips take the lozenge. She opened her eyes, and, sure enough, she still had all her fingers.

Flash nuzzled her shirt.

One thing you don't do, Phoebe knew, is refuse a horse who is asking for a treat.

Flash took another lozenge off her palm with amazing gentleness, then nuzzled Phoebe's hair.

She likes me! Phoebe was stunned. *But what if the heat gets to her?* It must be a hundred degrees in here. I couldn't get sunstroke when I needed it. No. Now they're going to find me unconscious in the bathroom with a horse that's eating menthol-eucalpytus throat lozenges slobbering all over me.

"Feeb?" Outside, someone tried to turn the knob.

"Amy!"

"I just finished cleaning up in there. What are you doing shutting the door?" The knob wriggled. "Feeb, the door is locked."

Nudging Phoebe's shirt, Flash snorted.

"Are you sick, Feeb? Are you throwing up?"

"It's . . . it's Flash in here."

There was a silence.

"Oh, Feeb. You only had to unsaddle her. You don't need to wash her."

Don't yell at the only friend you've got here. "She followed me in, and Heather and Tiffany kicked the brick away."

There was another silence. "Oh, wow. I just finished scrubbing that bathroom." Then the knob wriggled for a longer time. "I'd better get help."

"No! They'll murder me."

"Not if you didn't kick the brick."

"But I must have let Flash out of the corral."

There were more voices outside.

" 'Scuse me."

"Hey, who shut the door?"

"Sorry, guys," Amy said. "It's locked."

"What do you mean, locked?" a girl demanded.

"I have to go!" another girl declared.

"Sorry, kid." Amy was firm.

"I'm telling!" the first girl shrilled.

Amy sounded as if her face was right against the door. "Feeb, time is running out."

"I know. I think I'm going to pass out from the heat."

"Shower with your clothes on. That'll keep you cool."

"Amy, there's a horse in here with me!"

"Oh, right. Keep her draped in wet towels. I'll see if I can find something to pry the latch with."

Turning her head to get away from Flash's nuzzling, Phoebe edged toward the showers. For a minute the horse stood still, so that Phoebe got a look at all of her. She'd almost forgotten how beat down and moth-eaten the animal was.

"Oh, what the heck." Phoebe tore one paper towel after another from the dispenser.

Flash stood still under layers of dripping towels. Gingerly, Phoebe patted her shoulder. "You're a pretty neat old horse."

One thing, Phoebe thought, if anybody should come in and see me standing in the shower with my clothes on and a horse munching menthol-eucalyptus lozenges, they'd probably wire my parents to come get me right away.

She stepped out of the shower. It was, indeed, much cooler standing in the bathroom in wet clothes.

"Feeb?"

"Amy! Can you get us out?"

"Um . . . I think it's too late."

There were other voices outside:

"That's the one! That's the kid who won't let anybody into the bathroom!"

Then an outraged, unmistakable voice — Laurel's — said, "Rivas!"

Shaking her head, Flash snorted.

"Who's in there?" Laurel called.

Not answering would only make it worse. "Phoebe . . . Phoebe Townsend-Fanchon."

"*You*! What are you doing locking her in there, Rivas?"

"She didn't," Phoebe said.

"You locked yourself in?" Laurel sounded surprised but still dangerous.

"It was . . ." Telling would get Heather and Tiffany in serious trouble — and make me look like a total wimp, Phoebe realized. "It wasn't either of us."

The knob was rattled viciously. Something hit the door with a *thunk* that shivered even the frame.

"Wow! I never saw anybody throw a shoulder block at a door outside of the *movies*!" Whoever it was sounded awed.

"Didn't it *hurt*, Laurel?" someone else asked.

"Give me a rock." Laurel sounded like someone talking through clenched teeth.

As the clanging of rock on brass went on, Flash backed toward the rear of the bathroom. Phoebe went after her and stroked between her eyes.

"Somebody get Sumac," Laurel said at last. "We need a screwdriver and a hammer."

Flash whinnied.

"You can clown around in there now, Fanchon," Laurel yelled through the door, "but when you come out, it won't be so funny!"

As the banging and scraping at the door went on, the crowd outside seemed to grow bigger, and more restless. . . .

"I can't *wait*."

"Then go over there somewhere." Laurel sounded weary.

"*I'm not going to go out in the woods with all the wolves and beasts!*"

"*I left my retainer by one of the sinks!*"

Being locked, soaking wet, in the bathroom with a horse that was eating menthol-eucalyptus throat lozenges might not be the worst part of this mess, Phoebe realized. The worst part is that I'm locked in the *only* bathroom while over fifty campers are getting more and more desperate outside.

Finally, Phoebe heard Sumac's voice. "Are you all right in there, Fanchon?"

"She could starve by the time you get her out," Amy said bleakly.

Phoebe could hear the counselors conferring.

"We could try to toss Macaroni Surprise through the window." It was Cypress. "In a plastic bag."

"Never mind," Phoebe said.

The campers outside were growing more edgy.

"Guy! What if she *dies* in there?"

"I'm not going in there with any dead body!"

Cypress sounded grim. "Give me that axe and stand back."

"Eeyew! Eeeyew!"

Phoebe buried her face in the wet towels on Flash's neck.

There was a sound of wood splintering.

"Now the hacksaw," Cypress said.

The scraping of metal on metal went on and on, and then someone gave the door a great push.

A crowd of girls came spilling, shoving, into the bathroom.

And then they stopped.

"EEEEYEW!"

"There's a horse in here!"

7

The questioning was even worse than cold Macaroni Surprise.

"Why would we have put Flash into the bathroom?" Amy asked wearily. "Phoebe was scared to death of her."

"And what about the brick?" Sumac asked.

"I told you," Amy said. "If *Feeb* had moved it, Flash never could have gotten in. And I came along after the door was shut."

"You're saying the horse moved the brick?" Laurel demanded.

Amy shrugged.

"However it happened, you two seem to have a talent for trouble," Laurel said. "Tomorrow I want you to spend some time thinking about what could have happened if we hadn't been able to get that door open. We nearly had a riot as it was. You'll use the bathroom after everybody else has finished, as much for your own protection as anything. And you'll have meals in your tent until the other campers have settled down. In the morning, you'll clean the stables to remind you of what happens when you bring a horse into the bathroom."

"That means we don't have to go riding?" Phoebe asked.

"Oh, no. You'll ride. And then we'll have some lessons on how to close and latch corral gates."

Phoebe and Amy walked back to Tent Nine, pretending to ignore the hoots and whinnies and cries of, "It's that bozo that locked herself in the bathroom with the horse!"

Tiffany and Heather were waiting inside the tent. They stood close together, and there was something new and strange in their manner. They're scared! Phoebe realized.

"What did you tell them?" Tiffany looked even more anxious than Heather.

Suddenly Phoebe didn't care what either of them thought, or said. "You two. You shut Flash and me in the bathroom without even caring what would happen, and now you're afraid." She stepped close to them. "You almost gave my horse a heatstroke!"

"Did you tell?" Heather almost whispered.

"We haven't decided." Amy was stern. "Personally, I still think we have this legal duty, Feeb. People like these are a menace, right? What if they'd done it to some kid who didn't keep her cool like you did? What if it was some kid that got hysterical or something?"

Heather and Tiffany looked like seven-year-olds being yelled at by Laurel. Or by Cypress herself. Good old Amy, Phoebe thought. This is the best and smartest person in this whole camp. But she kept her voice solemn. "I can see your point, Amy."

Stephanie came bounding into the tent. "Hey, it's old Feeble, the horse thief!"

"You keep out of this," Heather told her sharply.

Tiffany inched closer to Phoebe. "We didn't *mean* anything."

"Sure you did," Amy said. "You meant to be rotten."

"Can you just think about it before you decide whether to tell?" Heather's voice was small and respectful.

Phoebe did not hurry to answer. "Maybe."

"Meanwhile, you'd better stay out of her face. And mine," Amy warned.

"And don't you even go near Flash," Phoebe added.

Bustling into the tent, Kelley staggered back when she saw Phoebe. "Wow! I thought I smelled horse . . ."

"Stay out of her face!" Tiffany snapped.

As the cracked and mournful sound of taps wafted into the tent, Heather and Tiffany got into their sleeping bags, silently. Even Kelley and Stephanie were quiet.

Phoebe woke at the sound of reveille. Even before the bugle stopped, she heard Tiffany whisper. "Phoebe? Have you decided . . ."

"She'll think about it," Amy said.

"It's just not right." Phoebe wiped her forehead with her sleeve. Cleaning stables was an interesting experience, she thought. It wasn't as bad as she'd expected. It even made her feel rather . . . hearty, like a person who fights forest fires and builds log cabins. Still, it was not the way she'd choose to spend every morning. "It's cruel, Amy. They have those horses out hauling kids around all morning in this heat."

"At least they're coming back to a clean stable," Amy pointed out. "And at least we didn't have to clean the bathroom."

Phoebe was not comforted. "It's going to be even hotter this afternoon when the Tenderfeet ride. Doesn't anybody care how a horse feels?"

As they walked out of the corral, Amy said, "We missed mail call."

"I've got all the soy protein I need." Phoebe shut and locked the corral gate carefully behind her.

There was nobody else in the tent when she and Amy returned.

On Amy's cot was half a bag of popcorn, on Phoebe's half a dozen peanut butter cups, with a note:

We each got a package from home.
H & T
P.S. Have you decided yet?

"We ought to show some class and turn it all down." Phoebe took a handful of popcorn and passed the bag to Amy.

"You are absolutely right." Amy handed three peanut butter cups to Phoebe.

At 12:30, Sumac brought in a tray. "Lunch."

"Thank you very much," Amy and Phoebe said solemnly.

After Sumac left, Phoebe set the tray on the floor. "What do you think lunch is?"

Amy glanced down at it. "Tan."

At one o'clock, Phoebe pulled on her English riding boots, but she didn't change from her sailcloth slacks.

Walking to the corral, she barely heard the whinnies and neighs from the few campers out in the heat. "It's even hotter than yesterday afternoon. None of the horses should be hauling around kids and saddles — especially not a horse as old as Flash."

"They've always done it, Feeb."

"That doesn't make it right."

As Phoebe and Amy walked into the corral, the Tenderfeet broke into guffaws and snorts.

"Quiet!" Sumac shouted.

"Birch had to go to town for hardware to repair the bathroom door." Laurel glared at Amy and Phoebe. "You Tenderfeet will have to get by with just Sumac and me."

Flash stood saddled in the hot sun, head down. When Sumac led her to Phoebe, Phoebe stroked the horse's neck.

Sumac made a basket of her hands.

"I can do it." Phoebe scrambled into the saddle on the second try.

As Laurel led the string of horses away from camp, Phoebe rode at the end, Amy ahead of her and Sumac behind her.

Phoebe turned a little. "Don't you ever wonder why you just go along with what everybody around here expects you to do, whether it's right or not?"

"Let go of the horn," Sumac said.

"I suppose you don't even care that there's a kid up there in trouble." This was true, Phoebe thought. Any sane person who sat on a horse in this sun was in trouble.

Sumac rode up beside Flash. "Which?"

"One of those near the front."

"Rivas, you stay with Fanchon." Sumac rode toward the head of the line.

"Amy!" Phoebe nudged Flash a little.

Amy pulled back.

Phoebe talked fast, and low. "I'm not going to

do it. They can make me clean stables. I might even get desperate enough to drink Yummoo. But nobody's going to make me ride this ancient old horse around in this heat." She tugged the rein the way Laurel had shown.

Flash turned to the left.

"What are you doing?" Amy gasped.

Phoebe nudged Flash with her knees, then hung on to the saddle with her legs and her hands as the horse broke into a kind of jog.

"We'll head back past the sprinklers on the Perrys' lawn," Phoebe told Flash, the words coming out more like grunts as she bounced in the saddle. "That'll cool us down. We'll have to stay off the road and keep an eye out for motorcycle gangs. But we'll find something. Maybe a church, or a sheriff's office. Then we'll . . . we'll . . . *we'll claim sanctuary*! That's what we'll do!"

She heard hoofbeats close behind. For just a second, her wish was so strong she imagined Flash breaking into a gallop, outstripping anybody following.

As if she, too, imagined, or maybe remembered, Flash began to trot.

"Oh, boy. Oh, no. Wrong way!" Phoebe hung on to the saddle horn with both hands. "Not the lake!"

When she saw the water ahead, Phoebe groaned, "Don't jump, Flash!"

It sounded as if the horse following was almost on them, now.

Flash trotted to the very edge of the lake. Phoebe closed her eyes and hung on with hands and legs.

Flash stopped.

"Good girl!" Phoebe scrambled to the ground and turned, all her hopes of sanctuary, or even mercy, gone.

Amy reined in. "Boy, are we in trouble!" But she sounded more excited than scared.

Between them, lifting and pushing and pulling, they got Flash's saddle off.

As soon as Sugar was unsaddled, Amy sat down and pulled off her boots.

Phoebe hesitated for a second. "*Pool* sharks, huh?" She took off her own boots.

She knew that there was really no escape. There was still the whole camp to contend with, all the rules, the counselors, the Perrys. She knew that she'd gotten herself and Amy into more trouble than she wanted to imagine. But at least she'd gotten the horses into the cool water. At least she wasn't doing something she knew was crummy.

As she waded into the water after Amy and Sugar and Flash, Laurel rode up, followed by Sumac and the Tenderfeet.

Phoebe was scared, but she couldn't help thinking it was an odd posse.

The Tenderfeet looked on, big-eyed, anxious, awed, as Laurel rode right to the water's edge.

"What are you *doing*?" Laurel seemed as much shocked as angry.

"We are striking a blow for . . . what are we striking a blow for?" Amy turned to Phoebe.

Phoebe thought for a second. "Horses. And us. We refuse to make horses work and sweat and suffer in the heat. We refuse to be the kind of people that make horses miserable."

"Out!" Laurel seemed to grow inches taller. "Now!"

The Tenderfeet stared at Phoebe and Amy and Flash and Sugar. The Tenderfeet looked at one another, confused and uneasy. The horses flared their nostrils at the smell of water.

It was a moment in which everything seems very, very still, and choices suddenly seem very clear.

Phoebe knew what she was going to do. She stepped closer to the shore, but not close enough to be seized by Laurel in a sudden dash.

"The way I see it," she told the Tenderfeet, "is this. Campers come here year after year, and do what they're told to do. The people in charge tell them the same thing year after year. Nobody thinks about whether it's right, or sensible. If anybody ever stopped to think about how the horses must feel carrying guys like us around in this heat, they never did anything about it. For that matter, I bet most of you never stopped to think whether it was right or sensible to make *you* ride around in this heat."

The Tenderfeet looked at one another nervously.

"Okay. That's it." Laurel rode closer to the water's edge.

Phoebe backed away, not the shadow of an idea of pond sharks in her mind. "Everybody goes along doing things they think they're supposed to. Nobody thinks about how the animals feel. But I'm telling you to see things for yourself! Look at the horses."

The campers looked at one another, and then at the horses.

A small red-haired girl near the end of the line slid off Lollipop. As she began fumbling with the cinch strap, the girl behind her dismounted and, without a word, began to help.

"Hey! What are you doing?" Sumac demanded.

Laurel turned in the saddle. "Stop that!"

The redhead and her helper looked at each other. Then the redhead shrugged, and they went on unfastening the cinch.

Phoebe could feel her heart thud against her wet shirt. This was scarier than getting on a horse for the first time. "See?" She patted Flash. "If enough of us say, 'No. This is wrong. I'm not going to do it,' if enough of us stick together . . ."

Here she was, the kid who dressed funny, the

only kid to get poison oak, the kid who got locked in the bathroom with a horse . . . and everybody was listening to her.

The mounted Tenderfeet watched the two unsaddling Lollipop. They seemed almost embarrassed by the sheer awfulness of challenging a counselor, but fascinated, fascinated.

"I am warning you!" Laurel told the girls who were struggling to lift Lollipop's saddle.

A few of the horses stirred.

"You guys know she's right," Amy put in. "She's not going to back down, so it's up to us to back her up."

A Tenderfoot whose glasses were sliding almost off her nose glanced around at the other riders. Then, shoving her glasses back onto the bridge of her nose, she took a deep breath and clambered down.

The girls around her seemed to exhale all at once, long and slow.

"Get the Perrys!" Laurel commanded, and Sumac rode away.

A girl at the back of the cluster climbed off her mount.

"Go for it!" Amy breathed. "Go for it!"

"All right! Everybody! In the saddle! Back to the corral!" Laurel ordered.

The girls still on horseback looked at her soberly, and then three more got off.

Helpless as somebody trying to herd grass-hoppers, Laurel rode back and forth yelling threats and orders at the girls who were uncinching saddles and staggering under them.

As the last of the riders dismounted, Lollipop splashed into the lake.

There was a great cheer from the girls unsaddling the other horses, and then beasts and campers plunged into the water.

In all the splashing and yelling and laughing, with the horses rolling and snorting in the water, Laurel's voice was quite lost.

Other girls came spilling out of the activity tents, hurrying from the archery range.

"What's going on?"

"Kids in the lake . . . and it's not swimming time."

"*Horses* in the *lake!*"

"And Laurel is *losing* it!"

Campers came rushing from all directions, now, followed by frantic, shouting counselors.

"Get back here!"

"It's not swimming time!"

"Who let those animals in there?"

In minutes, all the campers had joined those in the lake, while the counselors lined the shore yelling threats and commands.

"Do we have to come in there and *drag* you out?"

Phoebe threw her arm over Flash's neck. Eight

counselors were going to have some trouble hauling fifty kids and a dozen horses from where they'd decided to be. Still, it was scary.

"It would sure be interesting if they tried," the redhead observed.

Sumac came riding back, the golf cart close behind her.

Sumac dismounted and strode to the very edge of the water.

The golf cart stopped before it hit the sand. Cowboy Hank and Lady Lou scrambled out and hurried to the shore. Lady Lou wore a taffy-colored fringed skirt and a matching beaded shirt, and a lot of curly yellow hair, but her eyelids were plain skin color, and her eyes were squinty with alarm.

Cowboy Hank wore a cowboy suit, except for his shoes. It must have seemed like a real emergency to him, Phoebe realized. Otherwise, he would never have let himself be seen in brown loafers with tassels.

Phoebe leaned against Flash's shoulder.

"Fanchon!" Laurel shouted. "You and Rivas will be cleaning stables the rest of these two weeks!"

The redhead wiped her hand across her nose. "They clean stables, *we* clean stables!"

"*Yeah!*" roared the campers.

"And if I tell my folks you made us clean stables, and fed us the garbage we've been eating around

108

here, they'll probably sue you," a chunky brunette shrilled.

"And then you won't have *anybody* at camp next year!" shouted another camper. "You'll all go broke!"

Cowboy Hank and Lady Lou looked at the girls in the lake as if they were an infestation of ravening pond sharks.

"You'll have to live off Yummoo!" cried a girl next to Phoebe.

"No more Yummoo!" the campers began to chant. "Down with Yummoo!"

They were plainly having the best time they'd yet had at Big Tree, Phoebe saw. All of the indignation they hadn't even known they were entitled to feel came roaring out.

The counselors looked at Laurel, who looked at Cowboy Hank. Cowboy Hank looked at Lady Lou.

Taking a deep breath, Amy yelled, *"No more gray casseroles!"*

"We want . . . regular food!" another Tenderfoot bellowed.

Phoebe could see that everybody in the lake was getting carried away.

It was very interesting to observe.

"We want fruit! Fresh fruit!" the redhead beside her cried.

"Peanut butter!" shouted a tall, wispy girl who must have been at least a Bronco.

"CLEAN POTATOES!" Stephanie screamed.

This was greeted by a roar that would have shivered a tall pine, if there had been any.

Cowboy Hank took a step toward the water, but Lady Lou held him back. She raised her arms. "All right, girls. Let's all settle down and come out and dry off for dinner. Nobody will have to clean stables."

Phoebe realized she wasn't scared at all now. "Flash is too old to work anymore. She gets to hang out and take it easy from now on."

"*Yeah!*" the campers yelled.

"None of the horses work when it's over eighty degrees!" Phoebe looked Cowboy Hank right in the sunglasses. "And they get to come down and cool off on hot days!"

"*Yeah!*" chorused the campers.

"And nobody makes fun of how anybody looks!" Amy added.

"*Right!*"

By now, Phoebe suspected, the campers would have cheered anything she or Amy mentioned. She was tempted to add something like free long distance calls for everybody, but then she realized she didn't want one. This was something she was going to handle for herself.

Cowboy Hank raised his hand. "All right. All right."

Phoebe stayed where she was. "Promise. Both of you."

"Promise," Cowboy Hank said, and Lady Lou nodded.

"If you don't treat those horses right, we all go back in the lake," Amy warned. "And if we ever hear that you work them in the heat, none of us comes back to Big Tree. We'll tell anybody who's even thinking about the place how you abuse the horses. We'll even tell them about Yummoo."

"Okay, okay." Cowboy Hank looked very tired. "Now just get my animals out of the water."

The campers looked at Amy and Phoebe.

They're waiting for us! Wranglers and Broncos and Tenderfeet, waiting for Amy and me. Phoebe was astonished. At the same time, she felt a solemn sense of responsibility. "What's for dinner?"

Lady Lou turned to Cypress.

"It's . . . a kind of a hash," Cypress said.

No, Phoebe thought. No. If we come out now and let them shovel a kind of hash at us, they'll think this was just a flurry. Next they'll be serving Yummoo, and before we know it they'll be telling us we have to ride horses in the heat. I started this. I . . . And then the word came to her out of nowhere. I'm *accountable* — to the horses, and to everybody who backed me up. "Hash," she declared, "won't do. We want spaghetti. Mushroom sauce, no meat."

The redhead nodded. "And garlic bread!"

"Tossed green salad!" Amy called out.

One of the Broncos threw her arm around Amy's shoulder. "And garbanzo beans!"

It took Lady Lou several minutes to quiet the crowd. "Girls, we can't just make all that . . ."

Phoebe was not daunted. Phoebe was not a city person for nothing. "Send out."

"Or we all stay in this lake and never come back to Big Tree!" another camper warned.

Lady Lou spoke to Cowboy Hank, long and softly and urgently. Taking out his wallet, he called Cypress over.

"It may be a while," Lady Lou told the campers, "but they'll bring back your spaghetti dinner."

The smaller girls jumped up and down around Amy and Phoebe as the older ones crowded in to hug them.

In the bathroom, campers offered Phoebe and Amy dry towels and sunflower seeds and even bubble gum.

Cypress stuck her head in the door. "Dinner's going to be a little late. We had to split up and go to three different restaurants." She hesitated. "It's going to be *great!*"

It was. On the tables were cartons full of spaghetti with mushroom sauce, tossed green salad with croutons and garbanzos, and piles of hot garlic bread.

There was a problem with everybody trying to

sit close to Phoebe and Amy, but there was only a little shoving.

"I met Amy Rivas the very first summer she came here," the tall Bronco announced.

"Yeah?" Heather eyed her coldly. "Phoebe Townsend-Fanchon happens to be my neighbor. My mother drove her up here with me."

Tiffany leveled a look like a spear at Heather. "Yeah. But *I* never called Phoebe a bozo."

The redhead, who had elbowed her way into a seat next to Amy, stood up. "We want a campfire after dinner."

"But no dumb songs!" a Bronco said. "We're too old for 'Eensy Weensy Spider!' "

"Yeah!" everyone around her chorused.

A campfire is pretty nice, Phoebe decided, when you're sitting around it with people who all want to sit close to you, even if they do tend to hem you in. She didn't even worry about a spark flying out and burning her English riding boots.

"But who knows any un-dumb campfire songs?" one of the Wranglers murmured.

Cypress began to hum.

"What's that?" Phoebe asked.

" 'Laredo.' " Cypress sang the words.

The third time around, everybody joined in.

After that, Cypress taught them "El Paso" and "Shenandoah."

At last, Laurel said, "Lights out in ten minutes."

As the campers strolled toward the bathroom, Kelley said contentedly, "*Those* were campfire songs."

The redhead edged closer to Phoebe. "Do you suppose that horse tromped my retainer? I left it by the sink yesterday."

"It probably got squashed in the rush when you all stormed in," Amy told her.

"But it would be neater if I could tell my folks a horse stomped it in the bathroom." The redhead was reflective. "You know, I've never had a better time at camp in my whole life. You guys have to give me your addresses so I'll be sure to come when you're here next year."

"Where did you get your boots?" the tall Bronco asked Phoebe. "They look pretty classy."

Once in their tent, Tiffany told Phoebe, "We saved you and Amy each a chocolate bar."

Heather stood by Phoebe's cot. "You notice how we backed you all the way at the lake?"

"So what are you and Feeb going to do tomorrow?" Stephanie asked Amy.

"We're making macramé at the craft tent," Amy said.

"How about we come hang out with you?" Kelley suggested.

"You didn't sign up," Phoebe reminded her.

"We could go ask. This is the time, while all the counselors are in a good mood, and before everybody else does." Heather hurried out of the tent,

Tiffany and Stephanie and Kelley after her.

"You know what they're going to want to do?" Amy pulled off her sneakers. "They're going to want to make friendship bracelets to trade with us. I can just tell. And then everybody will."

Phoebe could not work up the energy to worry about it. "It'd be pretty funny if I came home with a whole armload of friendship bracelets."

"We can't fritter away our macramé, Feeb."

"I know."

"What we've got going is the greatest macramé ever made at any camp anywhere. We're going to leave it here."

"Sure."

"Every year there are going to be new, scared, nerd kids. Maybe they'll go to the craft tent. They'll see that macramé, and somebody will tell them about us, how we changed everything . . . at least for two weeks. I figure we'll be kind of a legend, Feeb."

"Can you be a legend at ten?"

"Around here you sure can."

Phoebe settled her head on the pillow.

"Have you ever been popular like this before, Feeb? I mean, in kindergarten or first grade?"

"It doesn't really knock me out now. We're the same kids we were this morning, when everybody was making fun of us."

"This is true."

"You know, we've got to keep coming back every summer, just to keep the Perrys and the counselors in line."

"You won't mind?"

"Not really. I have to keep an eye on Flash." Lying in the tent, Phoebe could hear the small sounds of bugs outside, busy with whatever it was insects had to get done at night. "You know, around the campfire, I was thinking that if my parents made a ton of money on this tour, I might ask them to buy Flash. Then I thought, where does a kid who lives in a second floor apartment keep a *horse*?"

"There are places to board her."

Phoebe could tell she was getting to the silly stage of falling asleep. "Boarding houses for *horses?*"

"Boarding stables, dummy. You go every day and look after her and ride her."

Phoebe sat up. "Yeah?"

"It costs a lot but . . ."

"Wow. You realize that I was hoping I'd get sick so I wouldn't have to come here? And my folks would have stayed home from the tour. I'm not saying they're going to make enough to keep a horse. I'm not saying they'll even consider it."

"But it's worth keeping after them. You never know."

"Whatever happens, you and I being here is the

best thing that's happened to Flash . . . to all the horses," Phoebe said.

"Hey — to all the campers. After they found out we could get a meal like tonight's out of the Perrys, they're never going to sit still for the garbage we've been getting. Feeb, with a friend like you I could — dare I say it . . . ?"

". . . *RULE THE WORLD!*" Phoebe said as she heaved her pillow in its flowered case at Amy's cot. Then she curled up, her hands over her head, waiting for Amy's pillow to hit her.

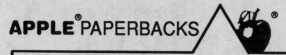

APPLE® PAPERBACKS

Pick an Apple and Polish Off Some Great Reading!

BEST-SELLING APPLE TITLES

❑ MT43944-8	**Afternoon of the Elves** Janet Taylor Lisle	$2.75
❑ MT43109-9	**Boys Are Yucko** Anna Grossnickle Hines	$2.95
❑ MT43473-X	**The Broccoli Tapes** Jan Slepian	$2.95
❑ MT42709-1	**Christina's Ghost** Betty Ren Wright	$2.75
❑ MT43461-6	**The Dollhouse Murders** Betty Ren Wright	$2.75
❑ MT43444-6	**Ghosts Beneath Our Feet** Betty Ren Wright	$2.75
❑ MT44351-8	**Help! I'm a Prisoner in the Library** Eth Clifford	$2.95
❑ MT44567-7	**Leah's Song** Eth Clifford	$2.75
❑ MT43618-X	**Me and Katie (The Pest)** Ann M. Martin	$2.95
❑ MT41529-8	**My Sister, The Creep** Candice F. Ransom	$2.75
❑ MT40409-1	**Sixth Grade Secrets** Louis Sachar	$2.95
❑ MT42882-9	**Sixth Grade Sleepover** Eve Bunting	$2.95
❑ MT41732-0	**Too Many Murphys** Colleen O'Shaughnessy McKenna	$2.75

Available wherever you buy books, or use this order form.

- -

Scholastic Inc., P.O. Box 7502, 2931 East McCarty Street, Jefferson City, MO 65102

Please send me the books I have checked above. I am enclosing $_____ (please add $2.00 to cover shipping and handling). Send check or money order — no cash or C.O.D.s please.

Name _____

Address _____

City_____ State/Zip _____

Please allow four to six weeks for delivery. Offer good in the U.S.A. only. Sorry, mail orders are not available to residents of Canada. Prices subject to change.

APP59